The Frog Earl

Also by Carola Dunn

The Frog Earl

Carola Dunn

Walker and Company
New York

First published in the United States of America in 1992 by
Walker Publishing Company, Inc.
Published simultaneously in Canada by Thomas Allen & Son
Canada, Limited, Markham, Ontario

Library of Congress Cataloging-in-Publication Data
The frog earl / Carola Dunn
p.   cm.
ISBN 0-8027-1203-7
I. Title.
PR6054.U537F7   1992
823'.914—dc20   91-31843
CIP

Printed in the United States of America

2   4   6   8   10   9   7   5   3   1

=== 1 ===

"IT'S GOOD TO BE home, Father." Simon strode forward with hand outstretched.

The Marquis of Stokesbury coldly looked his younger son up and down. "The proper greeting, Derwent, is 'How do you do, sir.' "

Simon Hurst, Earl of Derwent, stiffened and let his hand drop to his side. "How do you do, sir," he said quietly, suddenly aware of his mud-splashed riding breeches and boots. In the three years he'd spent at sea since last he was in Hampshire, the memory of his father's unbending formality had faded.

Lord Stokesbury's long, haughty face had garnered a few new lines and his temples were touched with gray. He was still in full mourning for his elder son, his black coat and breeches more suited to an evening in town than a March afternoon in the country. Diamonds sparkled on his lean fingers, an old-fashioned affectation he had refused to abandon when he reluctantly cut short his hair and exchanged velvet and brocade for Bath superfine.

"I had hoped," he said, "that you might see fit to return with due dispatch to England upon receiving news of your brother's death."

"I was in the South Pacific a year ago, sir. That's where Captain Hughes died and I took command of the *Intrepid*. Then we were caught in a typhoon in the Indian Ocean. I didn't hear about Cedric until we put in to Cape Town for supplies and repairs."

"So you are now a captain?" inquired a lazy voice behind him. "My congratulations."

Simon swung around. "Gerald!" he greeted the tall, elegant young man lounging in the doorway. This time his outstretched hand was grasped and firmly shaken. "Not captain, a mere commander."

"Ah well, I daresay your new civil rank is some compensation," said Viscount Litton sardonically.

"I've quit the navy, of course." He turned back to the marquis. "I'm ready to start learning how to manage the estates, sir, and"—he shrugged, feeling awkward—"whatever else is required of your heir."

Lord Stokesbury raised his quizzing glass. Once more he inspected his son's stocky figure, from muddy boots, past comfortably-worn riding jacket and loosely knotted cravat, to the square, firm-chinned face and ruffled sandy hair. He sighed.

"Alas, Derwent, it seems the navy has not quit you. I fear I cannot find it in me to face with equanimity introducing you as my heir. Litton, may I beg a favor of you?"

"Sir?"

"If it be not too great an imposition, pray take your cousin up to town for the Season and attempt to add a little polish to his manners and appearance."

Simon knew with helpless anger that nothing had changed. In his father's eyes he would never measure up to Cedric, the firstborn and always the favorite.

If Lady Stokesbury had been any more welcoming than the marquis, Simon might have stayed at home for a few days. As it was, when her son went to see her in her boudoir, she raised her lorgnette, shuddered, and said in a failing voice, "I fear it was a mistake to permit you to go to sea."

To his relief, his cousin was only visiting for one night on the way to London from Crossfields, his Dorset estate. That evening, Simon had his father's valet pack up all the clothes that had hung in his wardrobe since his last leave. In the morning the trunk was loaded onto Gerald's escutcheoned traveling carriage and the two young men departed in good time to reach town that same day.

The trunk might just as well have been left behind in Hampshire. In the course of the following week, Simon made the acquaintance of tailor Weston, boot-maker Hoby, and hatter Locke. His dressing room at Stokesbury House filled with new coats, waistcoats, shirts, unmentionables, Hessians, dancing shoes, hats, and gloves. He also acquired a gentleman's gentleman of impeccable references. Without Henry's assistance he was unable to don the tight-fitting coats or remove the tight-fitting boots; moreover, the little man was a wizard with a cravat.

Simon discovered that the navy's clove hitch and single wall crown knots were not half so complicated as fashion's Waterfall, Mailcoach, Mathematical, Oriental, or Osbaldeston. He admired Henry's artistry with a neckcloth, without being in the least tempted to emulate it.

As for Henry, he regarded my lord Derwent as a challenge to his abilities.

At last Gerald pronounced his cousin ready to make his bow to Society—and Society was all agog to meet the new Earl of Derwent. Simon was invited everywhere. To his surprise, he began to find amusement in the entertainments of the Beau Monde, though he missed the wide-open spaces, the camaraderie, and the feeling of doing a useful job he had had at sea. If now and then he overheard a whisper that he was not a bit like his brother, no one said so to his face and he was able to ignore it.

And then he fell in love.

One wet April evening, Simon was still dressing when Gerald arrived to drive him to Lady Bessborough's ball. Waving a greeting, he turned his head from side to side and grumbled, "Damn it, Henry, this collar is choking me."

"If the shirt points were only a fraction of an inch lower, my lord, I fear your lordship might be considered"—the valet took a deep breath before pronouncing the dread word—"unfashionable!"

Lounging in a chair to one side of the dressing table, Gerald laughed. "He's right, old fellow. If Henry didn't know to the last stitch what is acceptable, I'd not have hired him for you."

"Devil take it, I thought nothing could be more uncomfortable than getting caught in a storm at sea, but I'll be damned if a London Season doesn't come close."

"Your lordship's cravat," Henry murmured.

With a groan, Simon raised his chin. Mustering his patience, he bore the tedious business of having the length of starched muslin wound around his neck and tied with utmost delicacy in a *trône d'amour*.

During this process, Gerald continued the conversation. "You're not telling me you haven't enjoyed the past month. The *ton* has been falling over itself to welcome you like a prince, and you have succeeded in stealing the Incomparable out from under my very nose."

"Lady Elizabeth is quite the most beautiful creature I have ever seen," said Simon dreamily.

"My lord!" wailed the valet. "Ruined, quite ruined! I must *beg* your lordship not to speak while I am engaged in arranging your lordship's neckcloth." Ruthlessly, he whipped the cloth away and produced a replacement.

Silence prevailed for the next few minutes, until Henry pronounced himself satisfied. "If your lordship will condescend to lower the chin." His gaze did not waver from his master's throat as Simon pressed the creases flat. "Now a little to the right, my lord. And to the left. Excellent." He turned to Gerald, soliciting his opinion. "My lord?"

"It will do," said the viscount carelessly. "You know Lord Derwent's cravats are always limp by the time he's been in a ballroom for half an hour."

"My lord!" Tears appeared in Henry's eyes. "I assure your lordship I have tried every method of starching known."

"And his coat is wrinkled, his shoes smudged, and his hair ruffled," Gerald went on. "Don't worry, man, I'm not blaming you. It seems to be some irresistible force of nature."

Simon ignored this slander. "She promised me the first dance and the supper dance tonight," he announced. "Do you really think she'd have me, Gerald, if I popped the question?"

"Not a doubt of it."

"Your coat, my lord."

He braced himself for the struggle to insert himself into a coat he considered ridiculously tight and his mentors considered barely decent.

His toilette completed at last, he and his cousin set off for the ball. Limp neckcloth or no, Society had indeed opened its arms to him, and though he still thought it a shocking waste of time, Simon was enjoying the frivolities of the Season. Lady Elizabeth's kindness set the crown on his pleasure.

The Toast of the *Ton,* the Incomparable, a diamond of the first water, she had dismissed a score of suitors, including Gerald, to favor him, Simon Hurst, with her languishing glances. Nor could his father possibly object to the match. The only daughter of the Earl of Prestwitton, Lady Elizabeth was known to have a dowry befitting her station. Not that birth or fortune meant anything to Simon, entranced by her golden ringlets and cornflower-blue eyes, but it would please the marquis. For once the younger son was doing something right.

"Shall I ask her tonight?" he whispered to Gerald as they stepped down from the carriage and hurried out of the rain into Lady Bessborough's brightly lit vestibule.

"Why not?" Gerald responded as a pair of footmen relieved them of their topcoats.

Self-consciously, Simon inspected his neckcloth in a gilt-framed mirror hanging on the wall. It seemed perfectly all right to him. He smoothed his sandy hair. How did Gerald manage to remove his beaver without ruffling his dark locks? Like his late lamented brother, his cousin never looked less than impeccable. Nor, once he left his expensive valet's hands, did he ever appear to feel a need to check his appearance.

Following Gerald up the marble staircase, Simon envied the tall, athletic figure, the smooth fit of the blue cloth across the broad shoulders, the mirrorlike gloss on the black dancing shoes. Small wonder that Lord Litton had been, hitherto, the Incomparable's preferred suitor. Yet she had cooled toward the viscount from the moment that Simon was introduced to her.

He hurried on to claim her hand for the promised cotillion.

Simon generally threw himself wholeheartedly into his chosen activities—hence his command of one of his majesty's frigates at the age of twenty-six. Dancing was no exception. His version of the cotillion was decidedly energetic, and by the end Lady Elizabeth was fanning her pink cheeks vigorously, her delectable bosom heaving beneath blue sarcenet and blond lace.

She managed to find enough breath to say, with a flutter of darkened eyelashes, "La, my lord, there is not another gentleman in the room with half your spirit, I vow."

"That's because I alone have the joy of dancing with you, ma'am," he returned, pleased with himself for finding, for once, a neatly phrased compliment.

Reminding her that the supper dance was his, he returned her to her mother and went in search of his next partner. Despite his devotion to the Incomparable, he hated to see any young lady playing the wallflower when he could be standing up with her. Lady Elizabeth, of course, never wanted for partners.

Some time later, after the third country dance, he left a witty but muffin-faced miss with her chaperon and turned away to go in search of his beloved. Standing by a bank of potted palms, he was scanning the room when her melodious voice floated to his ears from behind the screening plants.

"I had made up my mind to let him kiss me on the terrace tonight."

"Oh, Lizzie, had you really?" Miss Jellaby's shocked squeak was unmistakable.

Simon's cheeks grew hot. She was going to let him kiss her! Was he conceited to believe she was speaking of him? He was too desperate to find out to do the gentlemanly thing and interrupt before he heard any more confidences not meant for his ears.

"Only it's raining," Lady Elizabeth continued, "and I feared he might turn into a frog."

"You don't really care for him, do you?"

"That clodhopper? Do you take me for a widgeon?"

Miss Jellaby giggled. "Jack Tar, not clodhopper."

"True. When I dance with him, I am in constant fear that he will break into a hornpipe."

"Then why do you not encourage Lord Litton? He is elegant, charming, wealthy, everything you want in a husband. I'd wager he was about to come up to scratch when you met his cousin."

"Lord Litton? My dear, he is a mere viscount. Derwent is an earl, and heir to a marquis, and the Stokesbury fortune casts the Littons' quite in the shade. Besides, he is so smitten I shall be able to rule him by raising my little finger. I should have him even if he really were a frog."

The courage needed to sail into enemy fire was nothing to the resolution Simon had to summon to walk up to the Incomparable and lead her onto the floor. He waltzed stiffly, and at supper found himself unable to swallow a bite. She chattered away, apparently unaware of any change in his manner.

Gerald, seated at the same table, was more perceptive. "What's amiss?" he hissed in Simon's ear as they all rose to return to the ballroom.

"Nothing."

"Cut line, coz."

It was useless to try to hide his angry distress from the cousin he had been close to since childhood. "I'll tell you later," Simon muttered, and hurried off to do his duty by his next partner. Would she, he asked himself, be equally delighted to dance with him if he were not the heir to the Marquis of Stokesbury?

In the carriage on the way home, the whole story poured out. Gerald listened in attentive silence.

"You should be thanking heaven for the rain," he pointed out when Simon's voice trailed miserably away.

"If it had been fine, you might have kissed her and popped the question. A narrow escape from a devilish fate."

"I suppose so. Nonetheless, you must admit it's a lowering reflection that my popularity in Society is due entirely to my father's rank."

"I wouldn't say it's quite as bad as that."

"I shall find it impossible to trust anyone's protestations of friendship. I'd best just go home and start learning estate management as I originally intended."

"Your father isn't going to like that."

Simon looked down gloomily at his smart, constricting clothes. "If I haven't yet acquired enough town bronze to suit him, I might as well give up and be comfortable again."

"God forbid. That is not the only difficulty, however. Cedric was never allowed to take an interest in the estates, you know, although your father is not an active landowner, as I believe you would wish to be."

"What do you mean? Wait a bit," he said as the carriage stopped. "Why don't you come in for a brandy and explain yourself?"

A few minutes later they were ensconced in deep leather chairs by a roaring fire in the library of Stokesbury House, with glasses of mellow amber liquid warming between their palms. Gerald sniffed appreciatively and took a sip.

"The marquis knows his cognac better than he does his lands," he remarked. "He leaves the management entirely to his bailiffs. As long as the expected revenues are produced, he asks no questions."

"He doesn't oversee his agents?" Simon asked, shocked. "If the captain of a ship failed to supervise his officers, there would soon be a mutiny—or she would sink. He is responsible for the welfare of both crew and vessel, as a landowner surely is of tenants and land. Is that how you run your estates?"

"Lord, no. It's not uncommon, though. I'll tell you what, if you are determined upon leaving town you had best go and stay with Aunt Georgina. Her bailiff, Wickham, is the best there is."

"Then why do you not have him at Crossfields?"

Ignoring this irrelevant query, Gerald continued, "He can teach you all you need to know. And Aunt Georgina will be pleased to see you. She always asks after you."

"As Uncle Josiah's heir, you must see a good deal of her, I daresay. I haven't visited Mere House in a decade. My mother was never as close to the old gentleman as yours was—only natural since she was so much younger than her brother and sister." Simon loyally kept to himself the thought that his revered mama had not liked the reminder provided by Sir Josiah Thompson that she was the sister of a humble country baronet. "Wait a bit!" he went on, refilling his glass and topping up Gerald's. "No one knows me there. I can go incognito."

"Why the devil would you do that?"

"Perhaps I shall meet a girl who loves me for myself, not for my rank and fortune." He sighed. "At least I shall know who my real friends are. But would Aunt Georgina keep my secret?"

"Undoubtedly. She would revel in being part of a conspiracy. You really mean to do it?"

"I shall ride up to Cheshire tomorrow," said Simon decisively.

"Ride! Good gad, old fellow, you'll be two days on the road. Hire a carriage, or buy one, or borrow mine."

"Frogs don't travel in carriages."

"They don't ride on horseback, either, to my knowledge."

"Oh, go to the devil, Gerald," said Simon with an unwilling laugh. "I don't wish to make a splash by arriving in style. And I'll have my *old,* comfortable clothes sent after me. Make my excuses to any offended hostesses, will you?"

Gerald merely shook his head, his expression foreboding, and finished his brandy.

The next morning, leaving a tearful Henry behind, Simon set out for Cheshire. The continuing rain had no power to add to his dejection. After all, it was fine weather for frogs.

=== 2 ===

THE MIDDAY SUN WAS warm on Mimi's back. The linden trees, their still-leafless twigs tipped with pale-green blossom clusters, sheltered her from the breeze where she lay full length on the old wooden jetty. After several days of rain, gray, chilly days not at all like the sultry thunder of the Indian monsoons, at last she was putting her plan into action.

Sir Josiah's butterfly net was perfect for catching tadpoles. Already five jars of the wriggling black creatures were safely stowed in Deva Lal's saddlebags. The sixth jar, half full of water, stood beside her on the gray, weathered wood. Before her stretched the calm surface of the small lake—the mere, they called it locally—reflecting blue sky and white puffs of cloud. With a flash of silver scales a fish jumped, then splashed back, sending ripples to lap gently a few inches below Mimi's nose. The tall rushes rustled.

Here by the long-unused jetty, the water was so clear she could see every pebble on the gravel bottom, though it was too deep to reach with the butterfly net. A school of sticklebacks darted past. Mimi briefly considered adding a few to her catch, but their spines looked dangerous. She didn't want her tadpoles stickled to death.

Extending the net on the end of its bamboo pole, she brought it up beneath a cluster of tadpoles. Compared to the sticklebacks they were clumsy swimmers, easy to catch, and she had quickly learned the knack of not letting them squirm out before she had them in position over her jar. Carefully she swung the net toward her through the water. It was heavier than it should have been, and she saw that she had caught a piece of driftwood.

She stretched out her left hand to remove it—and her bracelet fell into the mere. Sinking like a stone, it came to rest on the gravel, the glinting gold clearly visible and quite beyond her reach.

"Oh no!"

"What's the matter?" asked a voice behind her. A male voice.

Turning her head, Mimi saw a young man astride a bay gelding, gazing at her from the landward end of the jetty. She lifted the net up onto the planks, then scrambled to her knees and regarded the intruder hopefully. Males generally did what she wanted, and this particular male was not so well dressed as to object to a wetting for a suitable payment. He raised his hat politely, revealing short, sandy hair.

"My bracelet fell into the water. I cannot reach it. If you fetch it out for me, I shall reward you."

"May i ask why you wore a precious bracelet to go fishing?" he inquired in a skeptical tone, looking her up and down.

"I always wear it." She brushed at a damp, brownish patch on her pale-green morning gown—the train of a riding habit would have been horridly in the way. "It was my mother's," she added defensively. "Please get it, I shall pay you well."

"I'm not sure I'm ready for a wetting for a shilling or two."

"I do not mean a shilling or two." Mimi was growing annoyed. "A really valuable reward. I can afford it—I'm a princess."

"And I'm a prince," he said with a disbelieving laugh.

"You don't look like one."

"I was enchanted by a wicked sorceress. I'll tell you what, if you will promise to break the spell by taking me home to dinner, dancing with me, and giving me a kiss, I'll go in after your bracelet."

Mimi scowled at him. Of all the impertinent rogues! Then she glanced down at her bracelet, gleaming on the bottom. A fish was nudging at it. Perhaps she might reach it herself if she waded in, but then she'd have to ride home with wet, cold skirts clinging to her legs. Besides, an extorted promise was no promise.

"Very well," she said, tipping the tadpoles from the net into the jar as an excuse to avoid meeting his gaze.

He swung down from his horse and tied it to one of the linden trees. She hurriedly stood up as he approached. Though not tall he was strongly built, with a determined chin and eyes somewhere between blue and green and gray, like the sea in an uncertain mood. His riding boots thudded on the jetty. Afraid he might decide to take the promised kiss before he earned it, Mimi stooped to pick up the jar of tadpoles and held it before her as a shield.

"Simon Hurst at your service, Princess," he said, his courteous bow contradicted by his impudent grin. "Where is this valuable bauble?"

"Down there." She pointed, clutching the jar to her bosom.

"What do you have there?" He set his hat on the planks and took off his coat, a well-worn brown garment with plain horn buttons, and his neckcloth. "Did you catch some minnows?"

"They are tadpoles."

He raised his eyebrows and she felt herself flushing. Her annoyance increased. When she planned this unconventional outing she hadn't reckoned on the arrival of a mocking stranger.

"How deep is it? Can I reach it with my hand if I lie down?"

"I don't think so. The net will not reach the bottom."

Sitting down, he pulled off boots and stockings. Mimi quickly looked away, beginning to wish she had brought her groom after all. Simon Hurst close by, and clad only in buckskin riding breeches, a shirt, and a carelessly tied cravat, was a different kettle of fish from Simon Hurst safely at a distance on his horse.

He stuck one foot in the water and yelped. "It's bloody freezing!"

"You should not swear in front of a lady."

"I never swear in front of ladies. You are a princess, which is quite another matter."

Before she could think of a suitably cutting response, he lowered himself into the mere, grumbling as the cold water rose up his legs. "I'm not sure I asked for sufficient reward," he observed as it reached his waist. "Ouch! The gravel is deuced sharp-edged, and the ripples are distorting my view of the quarry."

Mimi decided that discretion was the better part of valor. "I'm going to put this jar in my saddlebag," she told him, and hurried to where she had tied Deva Lal, by a wooden bench under a tree. Quickly she stowed the jar and checked that the gray mare was close enough to the bench to enable her to mount.

She sped back to the jetty just as Mr. Hurst triumphantly waved the bracelet.

"I have it, Princess." He laid it on the edge and started to haul himself out.

Mimi seized it and slipped it onto her wrist. "Thank you," she said, backing away as he rose dripping from the depths, his shirt plastered to his muscular body. "Thank you very much." She turned and ran.

Safe in the saddle, she paused to look back. He was standing with hands on hips, watching her. Suddenly she was very conscious that her gown left her legs exposed nearly to the knee. Setting Deva Lal in motion between the linden trees, she called once more, "Thank you," and rode on, her gaze fixed straight ahead.

She did not dare trot because of the glass jars in her saddlebags, but he could not follow her until he had at least put on his boots. And then, she hoped, he would be more inclined to head straight for home and dry clothes.

How unpardonably presumptuous he had been to demand such an improper reward of a well-bred young lady! Mimi had no regrets about breaking her promise.

* * *

Simon grinned as he took off his sodden shirt, dried his upper half as best he could with his neckcloth, and put on his coat. He hadn't really expected the little minx to honor her commitment. The dainty gray mare and the heavy gold bangle, delicately chased in an elaborate pattern, alike announced the probable truth of her claim to wealth. Her voice was educated, despite a tantalizing hint of foreignness, more intonation than accent. And her small, gloveless hands were smooth and soft, unused to menial labor.

His thoughts wandered from her station in life. She had been hatless, too, her hair glossy as a raven's wing—a striking beauty with her cinnamon complexion and liquid black eyes. He had spent enough time in Indian ports to guess at her provenance.

Aunt Georgina would know who she was. He'd have that kiss from her yet.

Shivering, he pulled on his boots, mounted, and turned Intrepid's head back toward Mere House. The water soaking his buckskins started trickling down into his boots. He felt clammy, and more froglike than ever.

Fortunately he had not far to go, cantering across green pastures where contented cows scarcely raised their heads from the lush grass to watch him pass. The long, low house, built of pinkish sandstone, hugged the Cheshire plain, with the dairy block at one end and the stables at the other. When Simon dismounted in the stable yard he squelched at every step. The groom who took the gelding's reins from him snickered but did not venture to comment.

Baird was less reticent. Popping out of the butler's pantry as Simon strode squishily past, he said in a voice of deep reproach, "If you had warned me that you meant to go swimming, sir, I'd have sent Thomas after you with a towel."

"I'll inform you in advance next time I decide to take a dip." Simon was aware that the old man knew precisely who he was, remembering him from childhood visits. Aunt Georgina had assured him that her butler, as devoted as he was eccentric, would not give him away to the other servants, all of whom were new since his time. "At present," he continued, his teeth chattering, "Thomas would be better employed bringing hot water to my chamber." He handed over the soggy bundle of his shirt.

"At once, sir."

Baird's peculiarities did not interfere with his efficiency, so Simon was soon luxuriating in a hot bath. At moments like this he ceased to regret his life at sea, where a quick wash in a bucket of seawater was usually the best even the captain could expect. "Water, water, everywhere . . ." Coleridge's phrase floated through his mind, and that reminded him: What the devil did the Indian beauty want with a jar full of tadpoles?

He was unable to broach the subject at once when he went down to the drawing room half an hour later to join his aunt, a plump, gray-haired lady in her sixties who favored violet satin.

"Hot lemon and honey," she greeted him, leaving a letter half written on her little marquetry desk and joining him by the fire. "Baird tells me you have been for a swim. Is it not a little early in the year for swimming?"

"Much too early," he agreed, grinning at her affectionately.

"I hope you will not take cold."

"I doubt it, Aunt. We sailors are hardy folk."

"Of course. You must be quite accustomed to being wet. Simon, dear, I have been thinking."

Her loving nephew's response to this announcement was wary. Though he had only arrived the day before, he had already recognized that Lady Thompson's thought processes were not quite like anyone else's. "Have you, indeed?" he asked noncommittally.

Before she could elaborate, the butler came in, bearing a tray with a tall glass of murky yellowish liquid from which steam arose.

"Your hot lemon, sir." As he set the tray on a small table at Simon's elbow, one eye closed in a slow, significant wink. "Her ladyship recommends it to ward off a chill. Will there be anything else, my lady?"

Simon sniffed at the fragrant steam with a degree of caution, then sipped. The acid bite of lemon on his tongue, the sweetness of honey—nothing there to explain the significance of the wink. He took a mouthful, and realized that his tisane had been fortified with a generous slug of rum. Clearly Baird had his own idea of the best way to avoid a chill!

"Satisfactory, sir?" inquired the butler benevolently.

"Excellent," Simon assured him.

"Do go away, Baird," urged Lady Thompson. "I told you there is nothing more I require, and I wish to speak privately with my nephew."

With a disapproving sniff, the butler reluctantly departed.

"He always finds out everything anyway, but at least we can have the illusion of privacy. Simon, I believe you ought to change your name. Someone might put two and two together and guess who you are, especially if they know you were in the navy."

"I'd best keep quiet about being a sailor, perhaps. But neither Simon nor Hurst is an uncommon name, Aunt Georgina, and I have been so little in England these past years I doubt anyone will connect me with Derwent or Stokesbury."

His aunt sighed. "Are you sure you would not like to be called Sebastian Hetherington-ffolkes? You could keep the same initials."

"I fear I must decline the honor. Besides, all your staff thinks me to be your distant relative Simon Hurst, and I have already introduced myself to one of your neighbors. I was riding past the mere on my way to see Wickham when I met a rather odd angler, fishing with a butterfly net."

"That must have been Mimi."

"Surely not. Mimi sounds French, and this young lady was of Indian extraction, unless I miss my guess."

"Half Indian, you are quite right. Mimi is a nickname,

of course. Her given name—one can scarcely call it Christian! I believe she is named after the Hindoo goddess of wealth and beauty. Most appropriate."

"Her given name?" asked Simon patiently.

"Lakshmi. Of course no one can pronounce it, but then most call her Miss Lassiter anyway so it hardly matters."

"Lakshmi Lassiter. She is wealthy as well as beautiful, is she? She claimed to be a princess."

"That's odd." Lady Thompson regarded him with bright eyes, her head cocked to one side like an inquisitive sparrow—in borrowed plumage, given her violet satin. "Mimi is usually at pains to deny any right to the title. I wonder what made her claim it. She didn't by any chance have cause to push you into the mere, did she?"

"Good Lord, no! What sort of a loose fish do you take me for?" Simon explained about the lost bracelet. "She promised to invite me to dinner and to dance with me, as a reward." He thought it prudent to keep to himself his request for a kiss. "But she rode off as soon as she had her bracelet, leaving me bootless and dripping."

"I daresay she thought you shockingly presumptuous. If you *will* conceal your title and dress in your oldest clothes, you cannot expect young ladies to treat you as a desirable acquaintance."

"At that particular moment, she didn't precisely look like a lady. Why the deuce should she have been fishing for tadpoles?"

"I cannot imagine." There was something spurious about Aunt Georgina's innocent expression, and how had she guessed at once who his odd angler was? "Mimi has always behaved with the utmost propriety," she assured him.

"Who is she, Aunt? Is she or is she not a princess?"

"Strictly speaking, no, though her mother was. Her father, Colonel Lassiter, was in the Indian army. He was sent to put down a rebellion against one of the native rulers and then was seconded to him as a military adviser. The rajah took a fancy to him and gave him his daughter's hand in marriage."

"It sounds like a story out of the *Arabian Nights.*"

"Does it not? Of course, the colonel prospered mightily, in true fairy-tale style. When his wife died, he came home a wealthy man and last summer he bought Salters Hall."

"You know a great deal about him for so recent an addition to the neighborhood."

"Mimi calls on me often, and the colonel is a most hospitable gentleman. In fact, I have an invitation to dine at the Hall two days hence." Lady Thompson paused in sudden thought. "Oh, I have a simply splendid notion! She promised to invite you to dinner?"

"She did."

Their eyes met in a glance of understanding and complicity.

"EVER YOUR MOST HUMBLE and admiring servant, Miss Lassiter."

"Thank you, Sir Wilfred," said Mimi primly, accepting the slim young man's hand as she dismounted at the gate of the vicarage. At her wrist, between glove and cuff, her gold bracelet glinted in the sun.

"May I call this evening?"

"You know my father is always delighted to gather his friends about him."

"Too many of them by half," muttered Sir Wilfred, then cast a guilty glance at the vicarage. "Must be on my way. Until tonight." Top hat in hand, he bowed as deeply as his tight coat allowed and pressed a fervent kiss on her gloved fingers.

His inexpressibles fitting as tightly as his coat, he mounted his showy black gelding with some difficulty and cantered away down the village street. Sir Wilfred Marbury did not find it easy to reconcile the demands of the dandy set to which he aspired with the life of a country gentleman.

Mimi breathed a sigh of relief: he had not asked why Jacko was carrying a butterfly net. She gathered the train of her dark-blue velvet riding habit and turned to her groom.

"Wait here a minute, Jacko. I expect Miss Cooper is ready to go, but if she is not I'll call to you and you can tie the horses and go around to the kitchen to wait."

"Aye, miss." A short, wiry lad, Jacko was dwarfed by the three horses whose reins he held, but his worshipful eyes never left his mistress. She felt his gaze on her back as she opened the wicket gate and walked down the brick path between beds of nodding daffodils and rich-scented hyacinths.

On either side of the door, brilliant against the white-washed walls, grew polyanthus in every shade of yellow, orange, scarlet, crimson, and purple. These Mimi regarded with particular satisfaction—they were the result of one of her projects. On arriving in Cheshire last summer, she had discovered that the vicar's wife's chief joy was in growing flowers. Since then she had made a point of seeking out new varieties of seeds and plants and bulbs every time she went into Chester.

Of course, Mrs. Cooper had not liked to accept an endless stream of gifts she wanted but could not afford. A word in Papa's ear had solved that problem. Colonel Lassiter had begged Mrs. Cooper to rescue him before his gardener gave notice. His daughter, he said, having no notion of economy, bought far more than the gardens of Salters Hall could easily accommodate. Mrs. Cooper had smiled and happily agreed.

As Mimi raised her hand to knock on the door, it was opened by a fair-haired young lady in a slate-gray cloth habit.

"I'll be with you in a moment, Mimi. My mother went out, but Judith has a cold and could not go with her, so she will watch the children. I must just tell Papa I am leaving."

"I have a message for him from my father." She followed Harriet down the narrow hall to the vicar's study, pondering the injustice of life. To have opened the door so quickly, her friend must have been looking out of the window. She could hardly have helped seeing her erstwhile suitor departing in a hurry rather than calling on her as he would have before Mimi's arrival in the village.

Harriet never complained, always seemed cheerful, but she must be sadly hurt at the defection of all her beaux. Something, Mimi decided, must be done about the situation.

Knocking on the study door, Harriet went in. "Mimi has brought the horses, Papa. We are going to see Lady Thompson."

"Very well, my dear." Rising as Mimi followed his daughter into the tiny, book-cluttered room, he added, "Good day, Princess Lakshmi."

"Good day, sir." The first time he had greeted her thus, she had earnestly explained that, though her mother had been the only daughter of the Rajah of Bharadupatam, she herself had no claim to a title. She had long since grown used to his gentle teasing. "My father asked me to tell you that he'd like to call tomorrow morning to consult you about the orphanage, if that will be convenient?"

"I shall be at home at least until noon," the vicar informed her, "and I am always happy to see the colonel. Now off you go, girls, or there will be no sermon come Sunday."

The shortest way to Mere House, residence of the widow of the late Sir Josiah Thompson, Baronet, was back across the grounds of Salters Hall. Followed by Jacko on his sturdy cob, the two girls turned away from the village along a winding lane. Celandines gilded the hedgebanks on either side, and when they rode through a gateway into a meadow the greening grass was scattered with patches of pale-yellow cowslips. The air smelled of spring.

"There was never a day like this in India," said Mimi joyfully.

"We must go to the woods one day soon. The bluebells must be coming out." Harriet was abstracted, her thoughts on more serious matters. "Does the colonel really mean to found a new orphanage? Most charitable gentlemen are satisfied with sitting on a board of trustees."

"That would never content Papa. Like me, he must always have some enterprise underway. At home—in Bharadupatam, I mean—it would be an irrigation canal, or building a new village, or something like that. My

21

grandfather was forever grumbling about spoiling the peasants, but he was afraid another rebellion would mean having British troops quartered on him, so he always paid for Papa's schemes."

"And your papa always pays for yours."

"Yes, but my latest cost him nothing." She paused as Jacko rode ahead to open the gate in the next hedge. The paddock beyond sloped gently down to a pond and a fence-protected willow sapling, then rose slightly to a stone wall with steps set in it. At the top, where the ground leveled off, stood a small, white gazebo.

Deva Lal whickered as she recognized the horses gathered by the pond. They raised their heads and one began ambling toward the riders.

Mimi waved her arm at the scene. "I carried out my latest project this morning."

"The horses?" Harriet was puzzled. Mimi shook her head. "The ha-ha? The gazebo?"

"The pond. Don't you remember how the flies tormented poor Shridatta and Deva Lal last summer? Jacko said there were so many because it was a new pond—Papa had it dug for drainage and for the horses—and the frogs hadn't discovered it yet."

"'Sright, miss," the groom confirmed.

Mimi looked back. "And you told me all about frog spawn and tadpoles. So I asked Lady Thompson if I could collect some in her lake and bring them here, and she lent me Sir Josiah's butterfly net."

"I wondered why Jacko was carrying a butterfly net. You really did it? Frog spawn is horrid stuff. Ferdie brought some home once."

"I was too late for frog spawn," said Mimi regretfully, "but I caught lots of tadpoles."

"I'd a done it for you, miss," Jacko put in.

"It was fun. I'd not have missed it for the world. The only trouble was that I dropped my bracelet in the water, but a young man was riding by and he fished it out for me."

Harriet brightened. "A young man? Someone new to the neighborhood?"

"I have never seen him before." Mimi guessed that her friend was hoping for a new beau and was sorry to disillusion her. "He was *not* a gentleman."

"Oh dear. I hope he will not tell anyone about finding you fishing for tadpoles."

"With no hat or gloves and all on my own. But I get so tired of being always prim and proper! I suppose people would be shocked. I met Sir Wilfred on my way to the vicarage this morning and I was afraid he would ask why Jacko was carrying a butterfly net." Mimi's giggle was cut short. She stared at Harriet with an arrested look. "That's it!"

"What's what?"

"I have a plan!"

"Another one? What kind of plan?" asked Harriet, her misgivings obvious.

"To make all those wretched men start courting you again, instead of me. It should not be difficult, since they are only in love with my fortune. After all, you are prettier than me by far." Mimi deeply envied Harriet's fair ringlets, rosy cheeks, and blue eyes. "I wish I could give you half my dowry," she went on. "I have plenty for two, but I suppose that would be considered improper for some obscure reason."

"I'm afraid so." Harriet's laugh was somewhat shaky. "Does your generosity know no bounds, Mimi? As it is, I am indebted to you for my riding habit, my mount—a dozen things."

"If your mama had not permitted you to accept the habit, I'd have had to take lessons alone and ride alone. Except for Jacko." She flashed a smile back at the groom lest his feelings be hurt.

"So you somehow managed to persuade Mama that riding without a companion would make you utterly miserable. Not that I am complaining. I enjoy our rides and I love Shridatta," she stroked her horse's neck, "even if I cannot pronounce her name properly."

"You see, my projects always turn out for the best," said Mimi triumphantly.

"Tell me your new plan."

"I'm going to stop behaving like a demure, proper young lady all the time. If Mr. Pell and Sir Wilfred and the others disapprove of my conduct, they are bound to turn back to you, do you not think?"

"Mimi, you cannot! I know you don't care for any of the young gentlemen hereabouts, but if you lose your reputation no one will marry you."

"I'm not sure that I want to marry, especially someone who only wants my money. I'm quite happy living with Papa."

"You don't want a family of your own? Children? It is what every female wishes for."

"Well, perhaps, one day. Anyway, I don't mean to do anything so very scandalous, just to stop considering all the time what people will think of my actions. After living in purdah in India, England seemed very free, but you are fenced in by just as many silly rules and conventions, only different ones. Why should I always wear a hat when I go out?"

"Because otherwise the sunshine will make your complexion . . . Oh!"

Mimi laughed merrily. "You see? And anyway, it's cloudy more often than not."

"It does seem a bit silly when you think about it." The vicar's daughter sounded doubtful.

"To start with, I shall tell everyone about my tadpoles. That is not so very shocking, is it?"

"Not improper, to be sure, but rather eccentric."

"That's just what I want Sir Wilfred to think. I shall invite him to come to the scullery to see them."

"I thought you put the tadpoles in the pond."

"I took some home so that I can watch how they grow and change."

Harriet sighed. "Definitely eccentric, but I do thank you, Mimi. Only I cannot help hoping that the man who saw you fishing will not spread the story. I wonder whether he is staying in the neighborhood."

"I daresay he was just passing through." Mimi didn't really believe that. She rather thought Mr. Simon Hurst must be staying at Mere House, and she was not at all sure whether she wanted to meet him again or not.

They rode on in thoughtful silence.

Lady Thompson's butler opened the front door to them and Mimi handed him the butterfly net.

"A successful expedition, miss?" he inquired, taking it gingerly between thumb and forefinger.

"Yes, thank you, Baird."

"If you mean to take up angling, miss, I believe Lord Litton's tackle is in the gun room."

"I should not dare to borrow his lordship's rod," said Mimi hastily, remembering the tall, supercilious gentleman, Sir Josiah's sister's son, whom she had met two or three times on his frequent, though brief, visits to his aunt-by-marriage. "But perhaps I shall take up angling. Yes, that is a very good notion."

"Then I shall endeavor to find Sir Josiah's rod for you, miss, though I fear it is rather an ancient device, quite outmoded according to his lordship." He ushered them into the sunny, slightly shabby drawing room. "Miss Lassiter and Miss Cooper, my lady."

"Come in and sit down, my dears," said Lady Thompson, beaming. "Tea, Baird."

"And biscuits, my lady?"

"Of course biscuits. Plenty of biscuits. And do stop waving that net about. Was it useful, Mimi?"

"Oh yes, ma'am, perfect." Since becoming her neighbor, Mimi had grown very fond of Lady Thompson. She confided in her much more readily than she did in Mrs. Forbes, her own well-meaning but dull chaperon. Nonetheless, when she described her "fishing" expedition she omitted all reference to her meeting with Mr. Hurst.

Nor did her ladyship mention having a guest staying at Mere House. Mimi concluded, with a tinge of regret, that she was not going to see the impudent young man again. Guiltily she hoped that he had not had too far to

25

ride shivering in his soaking wet clothes.

A maid brought in the tea tray. Harriet was pouring when the butler came in with a fishing rod and tackle box.

"Good heavens, Baird, have you run quite mad?" inquired his mistress.

His dignity unimpaired, the butler favored her with a look of utter disdain. "I trust not, my lady. Miss Lassiter expressed an interest in angling, and I took it upon myself to offer the late master's equipment. Has your ladyship any objection?"

"You mean to take up fishing, Mimi?" Lady Thompson asked with lively interest. "An unusual pastime for a young lady, though not unheard of, and most certainly less peculiar than breeding frogs!"

"It is part of a plan, ma'am."

"Tell me."

"If Harriet does not object. She is concerned."

The vicar's daughter blushed but gave her permission, so Mimi expounded her intention of attempting to give Sir Wilfred Marbury, Mr. Albert Pell, Mr. Blake the lawyer, and the Reverend Lloyd a disgust of her.

"Then they are bound to return to their pursuit of Harriet," she explained. "It is not at all fair that they have abandoned her only because I am rich, but if they decide my conduct is unladylike they will not care for my money."

"That remains to be seen." Her ladyship sounded skeptical. "A noble enterprise, however, so long as you do not do anything too outrageous," she cautioned. "If you are quite certain, Harriet, my dear, that you wish to marry one of those fickle young men?"

"I wish to marry, ma'am, and it is not likely I shall ever have a chance to meet any other gentlemen."

"Very well, child." She nibbled absently on her fourth gingernut. "The colonel's dinner party will be the perfect moment to set your plan in motion, Mimi."

"It would be, ma'am, but I shall have to wait. Papa has a project of his own to propose. He is hoping to gain the support of the local gentry for founding an orphanage, so I must not invite their disapproval before they are committed."

"An orphanage, eh? Tell me all about it," invited Lady Thompson. Between them, Mimi and Simon were providing her with more amusement than she had had in years.

= 4 =

"IF I HAVE TO have Squire Pell on one side of me, can I not have Mr. Cooper on the other?" asked Mimi rebelliously, poring over the sheet of paper on the writing table before her.

"Sir Wilfred will be the only titled gentleman present," pointed out her chaperone, wringing her hands. "He will be shockingly offended if he is not seated next to you."

"But I want to offend him."

"Not at the colonel's dinner party," pleaded the Honorable Mrs. Forbes. The faded widow of the black sheep of a noble family, who had expired shortly after being exiled to join the East India Company in Calcutta, she had little expectation of being heeded. "He is not good enough for you, to be sure, and at another time it would not matter, but not at the dinner party, pray."

Mimi sighed. "No, you are right. I said the same to Lady Thompson yesterday."

"And your father wishes you to act as his hostess tomorrow. The proper arrangement of guests at the table is a *most* important duty of the hostess."

"You don't mind, do you? Not being Papa's hostess any longer?"

"Not at all, dear. I have never been quite comfortable in the role, but I hope I have taught you all that you need to know."

"I shall do my best to be a credit to you, ma'am. Sir Wilfred shall sit next to me. But I insist that Harriet is to be beside him, and Albert Pell on her other side. Mr. Cooper will have to go next to Lady Marbury, then, with you between him and Mr. Blake. Will that be all right?"

"So very difficult with a dearth of married couples," Mrs. Forbes dithered.

"At least both the baronets' widows are next to Papa, each with a parson on the other side. They cannot quarrel about that." Mimi dipped her quill and wrote in the names on her plan. "How complicated it is! Between that and the menu, we have been at it half the afternoon." She scowled out at the downpour which had kept her within doors.

"Pray do not wrinkle your brow so, Mimi. You will develop lines."

"I don't mind wrinkles, if they will only drive Sir Wilfred back to Harriet." Nonetheless, she hastily smoothed her forehead with one fingertip. "If it is still raining tomorrow, perhaps some of our guests will not come. I could not bear it if our numbers are upset after all the work we have done." Hearing a deep chuckle behind her, she swung around. "Papa!"

The colonel stepped into the ladies' sitting room. "I am come to upset your numbers, my love," he said, a smile creasing his thin face, made leathery by the sun of India.

"I hope you are teasing, Papa."

"Not I." Taking a seat on a flowered chintz sofa by the fire, he held out his hands to the flames. A lean man in his mid-forties, he was still unaccustomed to the chill of the English climate. "I have heard that Lady Thompson has a relative staying with her," he went on, "a Mr. Hurst, who ought to be invited."

"Oh no!" So he was still in the neighborhood! Mimi searched for a quick excuse to avoid extending the invitation he had requested. "There are no more ladies available to make up the numbers."

"What of Harriet's sister?"

"Judith is only fifteen, and besides, she has a horrid cold." Mimi joined her father on the sofa. "I believe I saw Lady Thompson's guest yesterday, riding by the mere.

He must be a very distant relative, I think. He looked quite commonplace, not at all gentlemanly." A true gentleman, she thought with renewed indignation, would not have demanded a kiss. He did not deserve to gain any of his claimed rewards. "And she did not mention him to Harriet and me when we went to tea." The news had doubtless reached the colonel via the network of Mere House servants who had relatives working at Salters Hall.

"I understand he is come to learn estate management from Wickham."

"Then surely we need not invite him? If he is nothing but a bailiff, he will not be in the least interested in your orphanage. Indeed, Papa, Mrs. Forbes and I have worked ourselves into a decline over the seating arrangements, have we not, ma'am? It would be too bad to upset everything."

"Very well, my pet," he said indulgently, patting her cheek. "After all, we have not been formally advised of his arrival. I don't wish to offend her ladyship, though. I shall tell her that the fellow is welcome to call at another time."

With that Mimi had to be satisfied, and she admitted to herself that she was not wholly averse to meeting Mr. Hurst again. Seeing her in her proper setting would teach him to be more respectful.

The following evening, she dressed for the dinner party with the utmost care. Since her aim was not to impress the guests but to persuade four of them to turn back to Harriet, this involved choosing her least fashionable gown, no easy matter.

Harriet, the daughter of an impecunious parson with a large family, would be wearing her best lavender sarcenet, newly turned to hide the worn spots. It really wasn't fair. Harriet would have loved to have pretty clothes, whereas Mimi was not particularly interested. The world was so full of other fascinating things.

Nonetheless, Mimi's wardrobe was full of muslins,

silks, and satins in the white and pastel shades proper to a debutante. When the clothes had been purchased in London, Mrs. Forbes had muttered halfheartedly that brighter colors better became her charge than these wishy-washy newfangled shades. At that time, however, Mimi had wanted nothing more than to look like every other well-bred young lady, even though she had no expectation of a London Season. Supported, as usual, by her father, Mimi, as usual, had won.

If she had since come to recognize that her chaperon was right, that the deeper hues allowable for riding dresses and pelisses suited her far better, she was not one to repine. She would never be a beauty in the English style, and at least she was fashionable.

Now, though, she regarded the contents of her clothes-press with a discontented eye.

"I wish I had had my saris made up into gowns," she pondered aloud, turning to the end of the wardrobe where the lengths of brilliant cloth hung. Asota, her little Indian maid, watched in bewildered silence. "Well, it's too late for now. I'll wear this one. Primrose makes me positively sallow, so it will discourage my admirers without offending anyone."

The pale-yellow gown was embellished with knots of jade-green ribbon on the high-waisted skirt and white lace trimmed the bodice and long sleeves. Asota helped her into it, then brushed her long, straight hair and pinned it in coils on top of her head. Mimi added a gold comb set with jade. She was completing the ensemble with matching necklace and earrings when Mrs. Forbes came in.

"Oh dear," she said, her gray curls bouncing beneath a lace cap as she shook her head in dismay. "I thought I had persuaded you not to wear that one."

Mimi giggled. "Is it so bad? That's perfect! You look very smart, ma'am."

Mrs. Forbes wore black bombazine trimmed with jet beads. Around her neck on a black velvet ribbon hung a silver locket containing a miniature of the Honorable

Maximilian Forbes, in a powdered wig. The only color about her was a touch of rouge on her flat cheeks, a daring gesture she made whenever there were guests expected in the evening, but always trembling lest someone should look at her askance.

Mimi eyed the pink patches with a considering air, then shook her head. Not tonight, she decided. She didn't want to shock anyone yet, not while Papa was hoping for pledges of support.

They went down to the drawing room, where the colonel awaited them. Realizing that it was her responsibility to see that all was in order to welcome their guests, Mimi looked around the room with its blue and white striped wallpaper and elegant furniture. A cheerful fire flickered in the grate; the woodwork shone; no speck of fluff marred the pattern of the gray and blue Axminster broadloom. On a side table gleamed an elaborately chased brass tray from Benares with cut-glass decanters of sherry, Madeira, and Canary wine.

Her father was watching her, smiling. "Satisfied?" he queried. "Or shall I dismiss housekeeper, butler, and all?"

"Oh no, Papa, everything is just right, but I must check the dining room, too." She went across to the connecting door and surveyed the long table with its spotless napery and sparkling glass. The butler, stout and stately, was giving a final polish to a silver spoon.

"All ready, miss. Now don't you worry, everything's going to go just fine."

Mrs. Forbes would have been shocked had she known on what friendly terms her charge stood with the servants. Mimi smiled at him as she adjusted the position of one of the narcissi in a faience bowl in the center of the table.

"Thank you, Waring. With you in charge, I know it will. Did you memorize the seating plan? I have a copy in my sleeve."

"No need, miss, I'll steer 'em right, never fear."

"Good. Oh, there goes the door knocker!"

The butler sailed majestically toward the door to the

hall as she slipped back into the drawing room. Moments later, she stepped forward with a gracious greeting for the first guests.

Lady Marbury's puce velvet gown, lavishly embellished with rouleaux and rosettes, clearly indicated whence had come her son's love of finery. Sir Wilfred decked out for an evening party was a sight to behold. Between hugely padded shoulders, his starch-stiffened shirt points threatened to commit mayhem at the slightest movement of his head. How fortunate, Mimi thought, that his chin receded. She could not imagine how he expected to enjoy his dinner when his coat was pinched in at the waist so tightly as to make breathing difficult.

His sister, Sophia, had also inherited the family weakness. Her gown was so extravagantly sewn with spangles that its color was barely discernible.

Dazzled by candlelight reflecting from the spangles and from Sir Wilfred's huge brass buttons, Mimi turned in relief to welcome the next arrival, Mr. Blake, the lawyer from Nantwich. He was followed by the Reverend Lloyd, vicar of Highbury, then Lady Thompson bustled in and kissed her young friend's cheek. In comparison with the Marburys, her inevitable violet satin, a lace-trimmed version for evening, was positively modest.

Over her ladyship's plump shoulder, Mimi caught sight of the impudent face of the young man who had rescued her bracelet.

"Oh no!"

His grin widened at her involuntary exclamation.

"Mimi, dear," said Lady Thompson, "I knew you would not mind my bringing my young relative, Simon Hurst, who is staying with me at present."

Mr. Simon Hurst bowed, all polite gravity now. After a brief struggle, Mrs. Forbes's training won and Mimi curtsied. With a curious air of guilty satisfaction, Lady Thompson moved on to speak to the colonel and to her arch-rival, Lady Marbury.

"You must be glad, Miss Lassiter," Mr. Hurst opened, "to be able to redeem your promise so soon, and without effort on your part. It is unpleasant to have a debt hanging over one, is it not?"

Baffled, Mimi glared at the wretched man. Honesty forbade denying the promise or the debt. While she was wrestling with her inclination to accuse him of taking advantage of his relative's eccentricity, he continued.

"Or, rather, the first part of your promise."

She would not give in! "Pray excuse me, Mr. Hurst," she said, attempting to convey haughty disdain. "I must have a word with my father."

As she deserted him, Sir Wilfred approached and introduced himself to the newcomer. His manner was condescending, yet Mimi observed that Mr. Hurst's response was by no means humbly grateful for the baronet's notice. She was struck by the contrast between them. Until that moment her attention had been on Mr. Hurst's expression, not his appearance. Beside the fop's splendor, his evening clothes looked disgracefully casual.

Of course, one could not expect a bailiff to be well dressed, she admitted, but nor could a bailiff expect to be seated at the dinner table with genteel company.

"Papa!" She drew him aside. "He will have to dine in the kitchen."

"I agree that those buttons are distressing," her father said, a twinkle in his eye, "but I cannot think it proper to relegate one of our guests to the servants' quarters."

"Buttons? Oh, Sir Wilfred." Mimi giggled. "Are they not amazingly horrid? I didn't mean him, though. It's Mr. Hurst. He was not invited, and he will spoil all my arrangements."

"How now! Lady Thompson has just been expressing her appreciation of your inviting her nephew at such short notice. I was surprised, but I made sure you must have adjusted your numbers somehow. There is some misunderstanding. You say he was not invited?"

"Well, not precisely."

"Not precisely?" The colonel's look was shrewd. "What are you up to, Mimi?"

"Nothing! Well, I did sort of promise to ask him to

dinner sometime. You see, I dropped Mama's bracelet in the mere and he fished it out for me. But I didn't mean for him to come today. You know I have spent hours arranging the seating."

"Now you know, love, that honoring a promise is far more important than correct seating plans! Besides, I'd not dream of asking a relative of Lady Thompson to eat in the kitchen, be he bailiff or baron."

"But, Papa . . ."

He was adamant. "You'll have to make the best of it, I fear. Tell Waring to set another place."

"Yes, Papa." When her father spoke in what she called his "colonel" voice, there was nothing to do but obey. Mr. Hurst would think he had won the battle, but he'd better not suppose that she was ever going to dance with him, let alone kiss him! Mimi drifted unwillingly toward the door to speak to the butler.

At that moment, Waring announced the Reverend and Miss Cooper.

"Harriet, where is your mother?" Mimi seized both her friend's hands.

"She has taken Judith's cold. I'm so sorry, Mimi, I know how hard you worked to arrange your table."

"That's nothing. Your mama is not seriously ill, I hope?"

"No, or we'd not have left her, but she is coughing and sneezing and quite unfit to dine out."

"Of course. She will be much more comfortable in bed with a hot brick and a bowl of soup." Turning to the vicar, she bade him welcome and commiserated on his wife's indisposition, then returned to Harriet. "Come and help me work out how to seat everyone, quick before the Pells arrive."

The two young ladies went to sit on a nearby love seat, ignoring the hopeful glances of Sir Wilfred, Mr. Lloyd, and Mr. Blake.

"What can you do?" Harriet asked. "It's by far too late to invite someone else to fill Mama's place, so your numbers cannot be set right."

"There's nothing wrong with the numbers. Lady Thompson brought Mr. Simon Hurst with her."

"Oh, Mimi, not the young man you met by the mere?"

"Yes, and without the least warning. So you see, the overall numbers are all right, but I cannot put him in your mother's place between Mr. Blake and Squire Pell. Three gentlemen in a row will never do. And I cannot simply move everyone up one place, for if Mr. Blake and Squire Pell are next to each other they will come to cuffs. Look, here's the plan." She pulled it from her tight-wristed sleeve.

Harriet pored over it. "How complicated! Can you not move Lady Marbury between them?"

"No, Lady Thompson and Lady Marbury must each be seated by Papa, with a clergyman each besides, otherwise one of them is bound to feel slighted. And you must sit between Albert Pell and Sir Wilfred, I insist. Oh dear, it wouldn't even help to send Mr. Hurst to eat in the kitchen."

"How can you even consider such a thing!" Harriet was scandalized.

"Papa would not let me," said Mimi regretfully. She looked across the room at the subject of their conversation. Mr. Hurst was watching her, and he smiled as he caught her eye. He really did have rather a nice smile, however disgraceful his behavior. She was glad he had not toad-eaten Sir Wilfred.

"You will have to move Mrs. Forbes," suggested Harriet.

"Squire Pell makes her nervous. I have it! Sophia shall change sides and Mr. Hurst shall go between me and Sir Wilfred."

"But I thought you had taken Mr. Hurst in dislike!"

"To be sure I have, but I need not talk to him. Only think how disconcerted he will be, first to be seated beside me and then when I don't speak to him. And Sir Wilfred is bound to be vexed, yet he cannot complain since I am simply being polite to Lady Thompson's relative!"

Leaving Harriet looking thoroughly confused, Mimi went to greet the Pells.

Mr. Pell, Justice of the Peace and Master of Fox Hounds, was a large, red-faced, loud-voiced widower whose wife, when alive, had always come a poor third to his horses and hounds. He invariably pestered Colonel Lassiter for information about hunting tigers on elephant-back. Bharadupatam being a good hundred leagues from tiger country, the colonel obligingly invented marvelous adventures to keep him happy.

His son, Albert, at twenty-three bid fair to follow in his father's footsteps. Large, clumsy except on horseback, he pursued Mimi with the same persistence he devoted to the pursuit of foxes, hares, and pheasants in their due seasons.

Those seasons now being past, he began to describe to Mimi how he had set his terriers on the rats in the barn. Hurriedly excusing herself, she escaped to have a word with Waring.

"Right, miss," said the butler when she had explained the changes. "Miss Marbury's to sit atween the squire and Lawyer Blake, and this Mr. Hurst goes by you."

Mimi glanced back at Simon Hurst, to find that he was still watching her, looking quizzical now. Perhaps seating him at her side was not such a clever notion after all, she thought. He might get ideas above his station.

She turned back to Waring, too late to stop his announcing, "Ladies and gentlemen, dinner is served."

$$=== 5 ===$$

THOUGH COLONEL LASSITER'S FREQUENT dinner parties were
not noted for formal etiquette, Mimi's attention was monopolized for some time by the gentleman on her right.
Mr. Pell was eager to tell her all about his "best bitch's"
new litter, "demmed fine pups," he averred, "all but the
runt."

Despite the squire's shocking language, as a subject of
conversation puppies were infinitely preferable to his
son's earlier choice of ratting. Mimi listened with apparent interest to his dissertation on deep chests, long shoulders, and well-let-down elbows, whatever those might
be, but she was constantly conscious of the gentleman
on her left.

On Simon Hurst's other side, Sir Wilfred, piqued at
being displaced from the position beside his hostess to
which his rank entitled him, was describing to Harriet
the latest London modes. Mimi congratulated herself.
There, at least, all was going just as she had planned it.
Mr. Hurst, however, seemed undisturbed by his isola-
tion. Far from showing any uneasiness, he disposed of
consommé and sole with a good appetite—and impeccable table manners, Mimi noted with a sidelong glance.
Lady Thompson's relative might be a bailiff, but he was
no uncouth yokel.

Mrs. Forbes caught Mimi's eye, reminding her of her
duty. She signaled for the second course to be brought
in, a baron of beef, a loin of pork with golden-crisp crack-

ling, and various dishes of vegetables. Mr. Pell, who had little use for soup and fish, was unlikely to say anything other than "pass the salt" for the next twenty minutes or more. Mimi had no excuse not to speak to Mr. Hurst—and she could think of nothing to say.

He came to her rescue. "I am surprised not to find mulligatawny soup and curry served at your table, Miss Lassiter. Most of those who live in India develop a taste for spicy food, I believe."

"I sometimes miss the curries," she confessed, "but not as much as my father missed beef and pork for twenty years. Neither could be eaten in Bharadupatam because some of the people were Hindoos and some Mussulmen."

To her surprise, he knew exactly what she was talking about.

"Cows being sacred to one, and pigs unclean to the other," he said.

"And Papa used to complain bitterly about the mutton. Now I am accustomed to English lamb, I understand why."

Mr. Hurst laughed. "Sheep don't care for the Indian climate, I daresay, any better than most Europeans do. You, however, were born there, I understand? Tell me about Bharadupatam."

Chatting with him about her native country, Mimi quite forgot that he was an impudent, infuriating intruder. He was amazingly knowledgeable, yet eager to learn from her, and she was flattered by his interest.

She realized she was ignoring her duties when the footmen, under Waring's direction, began to serve pastries, pies, and custards. After that she kept a careful eye on her guests and was ready to lead the ladies from the dining room at the proper moment. As they crossed the hall to the drawing room, she heard Sophia whisper to Lady Marbury.

"I wonder that anyone with so dark a complexion should wear pale yellow. Poor Miss Lassiter looks positively sallow, does she not, Mama?"

Mrs. Forbes cast Mimi an "I told you so" glance. Harriet squeezed her hand encouragingly. Lady Thompson took the offensive.

"I have always thought spangles quite unsuited to a country dinner party," she announced in a loud voice. "Indeed, even for a ball gown, one can have too much of a good thing. And puce is such an aging color, do you not agree, ma'am?" she asked Mrs. Forbes.

The chaperon muttered something incoherent and fled to the corner where her workbox awaited. Lady Marbury, seating herself by the fire and smoothing her puce velvet skirts, addressed Lady Thompson in an admiring tone.

"Your lace is remarkable fine for Honiton, ma'am. I'm sure I've noticed it any time these ten years. It simply never wears out, as Brussels and Valenciennes are so apt to do, being more delicate."

"Our English manufactures are of excellent quality, ma'am," Lady Thompson riposted, "and I consider it my patriotic duty to support them, especially since we are at war with the Continent."

"Sophia, go and play upon the harpsichord, pray," directed Lady Marbury, settling down to an exhilarating exchange of civilities with her adversary.

Knowing from experience that the two baronets' relicts would soon wear themselves out and snooze until the gentlemen appeared, Mimi tugged Harriet to a distant sofa.

"Sophia is a cat," said the vicar's daughter indignantly. "You mustn't mind what she says."

"She learned it from her mama, but she is quite right, this gown does not suit me. I wore it as part of my plan, but I must say, Harriet, that even for your sake I shall never put it on again. Besides, that was just an opening salvo. I shall bring up the big guns as soon as Papa has talked the gentlemen into supporting his orphanage."

"My father is helping him to persuade them. Only, how much money does the colonel need? The Pells spend all their income on horses, and the Marburys on finery, and I doubt Mr. Blake and Mr. Lloyd have much to spare."

"Oh, Papa has all the money he needs. He feels that if

the local landowners give their approval beforehand, they and their tenants will be less likely to object later to having swarms of destitute children introduced into the neighborhood. And Mr. Lloyd's approval will be useful in the parish of Highbury, since Papa has found a house there he thinks may be suitable. He has already written to Lord Daumier, as he's the biggest landowner in that area."

"A house in Highbury? Not Highbury Manor?"

"Yes, do you know it?"

"It's huge, but no one has lived there this age," said Harriet doubtfully. "It must be shockingly dilapidated."

"Papa hopes to buy it cheaply, which is why he wants Lawyer Blake's advice. Of all the gentlemen who came to dinner, only Mr. Hurst is useless to him, for Lady Thompson is already enthusiastic."

"Do you list Mr. Hurst among the gentlemen for convenience, or have you changed your mind about him? You told me very firmly that he was *not* a gentleman."

"That was because of how he behaved when first I met him," Mimi pointed out. "He has perfectly gentlemanlike manners when he chooses to use them."

"You were talking to him in the most friendly way at dinner."

"He is interested in India. None of my other beaux has ever expressed more than a momentary curiosity. Indeed, at times they seem embarrassed that I'm half Indian." Mimi's black eyes began to sparkle. "Ha, that gives me a splendid notion. But it's too late for tonight. The tadpoles will have to suffice for tonight."

"What do you mean? Tell me, Mimi," begged Harriet, but it was too late. Lady Marbury's slumber released her daughter from the harpsichord. Sophia spent the next quarter hour treating Mimi and Harriet to a detailed description of the gown she was having made for the annual First of June assembly in Chester.

By the time her father led the gentlemen in, Mimi was absolutely determined that one way or another she was going to outshine Sophia Marbury at the assembly.

Colonel Lassiter had an air of quiet satisfaction. His success was confirmed when the five young gentlemen clustered around the three young ladies.

"Your father's is a noble project, Miss Lassiter," exclaimed the Reverend Lloyd, his round face shining with inspiration. "To save so many young souls from a life of vice, and to lead them in the way of duty and religion."

Mr. Blake coughed dryly, his usual prelude to speech, which gave him time to review his words and make sure he was not about to commit himself irrevocably to anything expensive or actionable. "It is indeed a praiseworthy goal to remove beggars, vagrants, and thieves from the streets and byways and to apprentice them to honest trades and professions."

"Train the boys as valets, and the girls as abigails," proposed Sir Wilfred, taking up an elegant pose behind his sister's chair. Mimi suspected his tight clothes made it difficult to sit down, though his huge brass coat-buttons had been undone to reveal an orange and turquoise striped waistcoat. "Daresay I could persuade my man and m'sister's maid to give 'em a few tips," he went on.

"Paltry good-for-nothings!" Albert Pell snorted in disgust. "The boys'll make themselves useful as whippers-in and beaters, and the girls as kennel maids."

Sir Wilfred glared at him.

"I'm sure my father will consider all suggestions," said Mimi hastily.

Mr. Hurst's quiet voice seconded her attempt at keeping the peace. "It scarcely matters what trade the children are apprenticed to," he said, "provided that they have a roof over their heads and three square meals a day."

This point of view was obviously novel to the other four gentlemen. Mimi stifled a giggle at their blank faces.

"How very true, sir," Harriet agreed, gently approving. Mr. Hurst smiled at her.

Mimi glanced from one to the other. An alternate plan began to take shape in her head. Mr. Hurst was turning out to be a gentleman, and quite nice besides, certainly more amiable than Albert Pell or Sir Wilfred. Harriet would probably prefer being married to him rather than to one of her fickle former beaux. A match must be promoted.

All the same, it was too early to abandon her first plan. Mr. Hurst might turn out to be unsuitable or unwilling, in which case the rest of the prospective suitors must be there in reserve.

Mimi turned to the baronet. "Do you care to see my tadpoles, Sir Wilfred?" she inquired.

The effect was all she could have hoped. His mouth fell open. "Gad, ma'am," he stammered. "Tadpoles? Believe I must have misheard you."

"I expect your shirt points might interfere with your hearing," Mimi conceded. "However, you are right this time. I said tadpoles."

"But tadpoles . . ." His voice faded. He took a breath and started again, plaintively. "Little slimy, wriggling, fishy things? *Your* tadpoles, Miss Lassiter?"

Albert Pell guffawed. "They ain't fishy, Marbury. Froggy, more like. And it's frog spawn that's slimy. I used to put frog spawn in m'sisters' beds every spring until they married and left home."

"This conversation is most distasteful," declared Sophia, and with a contemptuous sniff she departed, unlamented.

"The metamorphosis of the frog is an interesting example of the mysteries of creation," said Mr. Lloyd.

Mr. Blake produced a cough, but no words followed. Even the Game Laws had nothing to say about frogs.

Mr. Hurst was regarding Mimi with a quizzical expression she recognized from when she had abandoned him dripping by the mere. Impulsively she said to him, "Would *you* like to see my tadpoles, sir?"

"With pleasure, ma'am."

"I keep them in the scullery."

As Mimi rose to lead the way, the lawyer coughed again. "In the scullery, Miss Lassiter? I own myself astonished that your respected chaperon permits you to frequent the servants' quarters."

"Believe Miss Lassiter is quizzing us," Sir Wilfred said hopefully.

"Indeed I am not. Come and see."

"Gad, no! Mean to say, won't do for all of us to abandon Miss Harriet."

Harriet cast Mimi a look of glowing gratitude.

At the door, Simon Hurst beside her, Mimi glanced back. Albert Pell and the parson were close behind. Beyond them, Mr. Blake, taking advantage of Sir Wilfred's unwillingness to risk sitting down, was sharing the sofa with Harriet.

Two out of four, she thought triumphantly. Not bad for her first effort.

"I've been racking my brains trying to guess why you were fishing for tadpoles," said Mr. Hurst. "Was it simply for the pleasure of watching them grow and change?"

"No, for the horses."

He looked startled. "You don't mean that in India horses are fed on tadpoles?"

"Only the fiercest chargers," she teased, laughing. "No, of course not. I put most of them in the new pond in the paddock so that the frogs will eat the flies that bite the horses."

"I'm glad to hear that the frogs are the heroes of your story."

His voice held an undertone of bitterness. Mimi was inclined to investigate, but they had reached the kitchen. As she opened the door, the servants, seated around the table demolishing the remains of the roasts, stared in dismay at this invasion by the quality. One or two went on chewing stolidly, some froze with their mouths open and their forks in midair, and several began to scramble to their feet.

"Oh, I'm sorry!" said Mimi, equally dismayed. She stopped in the doorway, blocking it. "I had not considered that this is an inconvenient time."

Cook, a tall, solid Yorkshirewoman, rose majestically from the end of the table. "Tha's always welcome, lass, but there's no denying 'tis not t' best moment."

"No, I daresay the tadpoles are hidden by stacks of dirty dishes. Please don't disturb yourselves, everyone." She turned to the gentlemen. "I cannot show you tonight after all. I hope you are not excessively disappointed."

Mr. Lloyd looked relieved.

"Demme if I'll be tossed at the fence by a bunch of demmed servants!" Albert Pell roared, as if he really wanted to see the tadpoles. He must, as usual, have imbibed a trifle too much port. Mimi hurriedly pulled the kitchen door shut behind her.

Mr. Hurst grinned at her. "Oh, but I *am* excessively disappointed. Still, I expect it will be easier to inspect them by daylight. May I call tomorrow, Miss Lassiter?"

"By all means, sir," she said, deciding that Harriet must spend the day at Salters Hall tomorrow, if her mother could possibly spare her from her chores.

Mrs. Prestwick popped out of the housekeeper's room to see what the commotion in the passage was about. While Mimi explained, Mr. Hurst urged a sulky Albert Pell on toward the drawing room, with the parson following them. The apprentice bailiff had a commanding way about him, Mimi noted gratefully.

"Pray ask Waring to bring the tea tray," she went on, suddenly weary. "It's not too early, is it?"

"No, Miss Mimi, not a minute too early, with you looking fagged half to death."

"I expect most of that is due to this wretched gown, but I am a little tired, I own. I had not realized acting as hostess was such hard work, and I fear I've made a sad mull of it."

"Now never you mind, lovey. There's none of them going to turn down the colonel's hospitality just because everything didn't go smooth as silk, believe you me. Off you go and keep them happy another half an hour, and that Asota'll have your bed warmed and ready for you."

"Thank you, Mrs. Prestwick," Mimi said, and hurried after her guests.

As if to assure her that their defection was momentary, Sir Wilfred and Mr. Blake hovered over her while she poured the tea. The baronet stood at her side, complimenting her lavishly if uninventively on the grace with which she performed this exercise. At least the lawyer made himself useful distributing cups of tea to the company. Annoyed with them for deserting Harriet, Mimi found it difficult to be polite. Unfortunately, they took her shortness as the result of pique at their lack of interest in her tadpoles.

"Fascinating things, frogs," Sir Wilfred vowed. "Take my oath, always found 'em . . . er . . . fascinating."

Mr. Blake coughed. "Beyond any reasonable doubt, the scullery must be considered the most logical location for the maintenance of livestock . . . er . . . domestic . . . er . . . creatures of that sort. As a lawyer, I have a particular appreciation of the logical solution."

Botheration, Mimi thought, the tadpoles were obviously not going to be much help as a means of detaching her unwanted beaux.

Albert was sulking in a corner, having refused tea; Mr. Lloyd was talking to his fellow clergyman, Mr. Cooper; but Simon Hurst had taken the place on the sofa beside Harriet and was saying something that made her laugh.

That was definitely a hopeful sign—so why was Mimi not quite sure that their evident harmony pleased her?

=== 6 ===

"So YOU ACHIEVED YOUR promised invitation to dinner," said Lady Thompson as the carriage set off down the drive. "I fear, however, you must find our country entertainments dull work after the splendors of London?"

Settling back against the old-fashioned landau's comfortable cushions, Simon smiled at her inquiring tone. "On the contrary, Aunt." His back to the horses, he watched Salters Hall recede, the black-on-white diamond and rosette pattern of its half-timbering sharply defined in the moonlight.

"So you enjoyed the party?"

"I found it most amusing. Your princess is a little baggage. She did her best to persuade her father not to receive me, I believe, but I daresay I shall count that promise as fulfilled."

"Pray do, Simon. I can scarcely take you to the Lassiters' again uninvited, now that you are known in the neighborhood."

"No fear of that—Miss Mimi and I have cried friends. What on earth possessed her to invite her multitudinous admirers to view her tadpoles?"

"I cannot imagine, I vow. Is that where you all went off to?"

As once before, when he asked her what Mimi wanted with the tadpoles, Simon had the impression that Aunt Georgina was not being totally frank. No matter; doubtless the girl had an equally original yet oddly reasonable purpose in mind tonight.

"We were headed for the scullery," he told his aunt, "but the servants were dining, so we turned back. I requested permission to call tomorrow to see the wretched creatures, deuced if I know why. The cook called her 'lass,'" he added irrelevantly, "and the housekeeper called her 'lovey.'"

Lady Thompson chuckled. "She's an engaging child. She has quite won over Baird, you know. It is a great pity that all the local chuckleheads are interested only in her fortune."

An engaging child? mused Simon later, shrugging off his coat and slinging it over the back of the chair by his bed in a way that would have appalled Henry. His crumpled cravat he tossed on the dressing table as he kicked off his shoes.

Miss Lakshmi Lassiter was indubitably engaging, but her childlike, innocent naughtiness was contradicted by her delightfully womanly figure. Not for a moment did he credit that her beaux had eyes only for her money. It might be entertaining to give them a little competition—if Lady Elizabeth had not irreparably broken his heart.

Climbing into the high four-poster, he waited for the familiar wave of humiliated misery to sweep over him. And waited. He summoned up a tormenting vision of golden ringlets, alabaster brow, rose-petal cheeks, and white shoulders. Somehow he couldn't get her nose quite right, nor recall the precise shade of her eyes. Blue eyes were really rather commonplace, he decided as he drifted into sleep.

A light drizzle was falling early the next morning when Simon rode off to take breakfast with Wickham and his hospitable wife. Lady Thompson had instructed her overseer, a short, taciturn man, to teach her young relative estate management, and he had willingly taken on the task. For the better part of three days, Simon had ridden about with him, discussing drainage and breeds of cattle, crop rotation, and ways to persuade tenant farmers to use modern agricultural methods.

Simon had learned enough to realize that he was not learning what he needed to know.

The Marquis of Stokesbury owned five estates in various parts of the country besides his principal seat in Hampshire. Of the six, the four largest were entailed and would come to Simon with the title whether his father thought him an adequate heir or no. One man could not possibly supervise the day-to-day detail of a score or more farms in such different areas as the orchards and hopfields of Kent and the high, sheep-rearing fells of Westmorland.

As Gerald had suggested, Simon needed to be able to oversee the overseers. Taking his seat at the table in the Wickhams' cozy kitchen, he spread a slice of bread still warm from the oven with rich yellow butter from the Home Farm, and tried to explain.

"You see, what I must be able to judge is not merely whether to send more milk to market or make it into cheese, but whether the estate is being run honestly and competently."

"Does her ladyship not trust me after all these years?" Mr. Wickham interrupted, puzzled and suspicious.

"Of course she does, sir. I don't mean the Mere House estate."

"Then just what do ye mean?"

"Let the lad eat, Bill," said his wife, heaping Simon's plate with eggs, crisp rashers of bacon, a couple of plump brown sausages, and bread fried in the drippings.

Banishing memories of sea biscuit washed down with long-stored, greenish water, he set to and for some time was unable to continue his explanation. Mrs. Wickham beamed with satisfaction and pushed a pot of homemade strawberry jam toward him.

"Thank you, ma'am, I couldn't eat another bite," he said, taking a draft of ale and pushing back his chair. "I shan't need any dinner tonight."

"Just what do ye mean, lad?" persisted the bailiff, still troubled. "I don't like the notion o' teaching ye to be poking and prying into some poor soul's business."

"It'll be my own business," Simon assured him incautiously.

Wickham frowned. "Ye've an estate o' your own, then? And a man to manage it for ye?"

"Oh hell! I can see I'll have to confess. Pardon my language, Mrs. Wickham, but I didn't want anyone to know who I am."

She refilled his glass. "And who might that be, lad?"

"As a matter of fact, I'm Lord Derwent. Sir Josiah was my mother's elder brother—and my father is the Marquis of Stokesbury."

"If I didn't think you've an air of authority about you for a lad with his way to make in the world," marveled Mrs. Wickham.

"I was an officer in the navy," said Simon, abashed. He told them how he had become Earl of Derwent on his brother's death, and they murmured condolences.

"Seems to me it's the marquis's job to show ye how to go on, my lord," said Wickham doubtfully.

"Please, don't call me that. Mr. Hurst, if you like, but 'lad' will do very well." He smiled at Mrs. Wickham. How was he to avoid revealing that his father was a negligent landlord who despised his new heir? "The marquis is a busy man. My cousin, Lord Litton, suggested that I couldn't do better than to learn from you, sir."

"I've a high opinion o' Lord Litton," grunted Wickham. "If his lordship wants me to give ye a hand, I'll do it, and keep my mouth shut too. And so will ye, mind, Bess," he admonished his wife.

"Thank you, both of you." Going off with the bailiff to set about the morning's studies, he wondered whether it was nonsensical to insist on keeping his incognito. No, if his true identity was revealed, his aunt's neighbors would be offended at being deceived—and no doubt they would expect him to start dressing and behaving like an earl. He had had enough of attempting that in London.

Besides, he wanted his dance and kiss from the princess before she found out who he really was.

Some six hours later, he saddled his horse and set off

to call at Salters Hall. It was still raining, but after Wickham's stuffy office the air was clear and fresh and Simon was glad to be outside. Besides, rain made it more likely that Miss Lassiter would be at home, he thought, cantering past the mere and across the flat green pastures. He did not flatter himself that the prospect of his visit at an unspecified hour would have detained her.

Rather than going around by the lanes, as the carriage had, he had asked Wickham for directions across the fields. His bay gelding, Intrepid, was no hunter so every gate had to be opened, then shut behind them.

He was performing this task when he realized that the paddock before him must be the one his hostess had referred to last night. The pond in the hollow had a raw, new look, without reeds or other water plants, only a solitary golden-green willow sapling growing to one side. A gray heron hunched near the edge. Three horses stood beneath a chestnut at the far end of the field, staring at the strangers but showing no disposition to leave their shelter to investigate.

Miss Lassiter might be pleased with a report on the progress of her liberated tadpoles. He rode down to the pond, reined in Intrepid on the muddy, hoof-trampled bank, and dismounted.

The heron fixed him with a beady eye, flexed its wide, arched wings, and flew off with an indignant honk. As the ripples of its departure faded, Simon saw that the raindrops plinking into the pond made it impossible to see beneath the surface. Remounting, he rode on.

The Lassiters' butler admitted grudgingly that his mistress was at home, but he made no move to invite Simon in. His gaze appeared to be fixed on the floor. Puzzled, Simon glanced down. His boots had picked up a generous quantity of mud by the pond, and even as he looked, a small clod broke off.

His laugh was rueful. Surely no one would believe he was a nobleman if he tried to claim it! "Since I am come to see Miss Lassiter's tadpoles, perhaps I had best go straight round to the kitchen door, if you will kindly direct me thither and inform her of my arrival."

"That won't be necessary, sir." The butler's manner thawed somewhat. "May I suggest that I call a footman to remove the boots and give them a quick cleaning before I show you to the drawing room."

This expedient being adopted, Simon was ushered into Miss Lassiter's presence a quarter hour later with nothing worse than a sort of tidemark around his ankles.

The young lady's dark head was bowed over a piece of needlework. On hearing his name announced, she looked up and smiled.

"How do you do, Mr. Hurst," she said demurely. "How kind of you to visit us in this sadly damp weather. You met Mrs. Forbes last night, of course."

He bowed to the faded chaperon with a vague recollection of having been introduced. "Of course. How do you do, ma'am. I trust I find you well?"

"Well enough, thank you, Mr. Hurst." She set down her knitting, some garment of indeterminate color and inordinate length, and withdrew a skein of yarn from her workbox.

"Pray be seated, sir," said Miss Lassiter. "Ma'am, do you wish me to hold the wool while you roll a ball?"

"I hesitate to ask it when we have a caller, Mimi, but if you wouldn't mind . . ."

"Not at all." She began to fold her own work.

"You are already occupied. Allow me to be of assistance," Simon offered, sitting down beside Mrs. Forbes. To his disappointment, the Indian princess was behaving today as sedately as any well-bred milk-and-water miss, but he decided to play up to her lead. Perhaps she had been raked over the coals for her unseemly liveliness last night, though he had thought her to have more spirit than to be cowed by a scolding. He took the skein from Mrs. Forbes. "You will have to show me what to do for you, ma'am."

"So kind."

Patiently he followed her muddled instructions until he had the yarn settled around each hand and stretched between them. She began to wind the ball, and at last he had attention to spare for Miss Lassiter.

She was watching him with wickedly sparkling black eyes, her lips pressed together so firmly he knew she was trying to hide her amusement. She was saucy Mimi again, not the decorous Miss Lassiter. Oddly reassured, he came to the conclusion that gentlemen callers did not as a rule offer their services for winding wool. If Gerald had foreseen the possibility, no doubt he would have warned against it. Simon sighed.

"I trust you are not regretting your kindness already, Mr. Hurst?"

"Certainly not, Miss Lassiter." There was a jerk on his hands and he nearly dropped the lot.

Mimi let fall her own work. "Oh dear, you must not hold it so taut. And you need to move your hands just the tiniest bit, in rhythm with Mrs. Forbes's winding. Here, let me show you."

She was at his side, her little hands holding his wrists. He breathed in the warm, rich smell of her smooth skin. For a moment he was as breathless as if he were drowning in her fragrance—then he recalled that she was a princess and he was a frog. Frogs don't drown. He surfaced as she giggled.

"Heavens, it's much easier to do than to demonstrate. Perhaps I should . . ."

"Sir Wilfred, ma'am," announced the butler.

With a startled jerk, she moved away from Simon, then stepped forward to greet the baronet. Today the young man was dressed less like a popinjay. In fact, Simon suspected that Gerald would have approved of his garb, except for a shudder at the pink roses embroidered on his blue waistcoat. His coat was tight-fitting but neither padded at the shoulders nor pinched in at the waist, and his boots had an admirable gloss.

Simon glanced down regretfully at his own footwear.

"Servant, Mrs. Forbes. Servant—ah—Hurst." Sir Wilfred raised contemptuous eyebrows at the sight of the yarn linking the two.

Feeling foolish, Simon nodded in acknowledgment of the greeting. "You'll excuse my shaking your hand, Sir Wilfred," he said dryly.

"I was about to take Mr. Hurst to see my tadpoles," said Mimi. Gone without a trace was the demure young lady who had so recently labored at her needlework. "I hope you have reconsidered your decision, Sir Wilfred, and will go with us?"

"Er . . . better not." The baronet looked round for inspiration, then produced an unconvincing sneeze. "Atchoo! Slight cold coming on, don't you know."

"Then you ought not to be out in this weather. I hope you don't mean to pass it on to the rest of us, Sir Wilfred," said Mimi severely, to Simon's utter delight.

"No, no, assure you, ma'am. Nothing to it, be better directly. All the same, best not to risk it, standing in the damp on a cold stone floor, don't you know. Daresay Hurst will like to take himself so you won't be obliged to desert a guest."

"Mr. Hurst is as much my guest as you are, sir. If you don't care to come, I daresay you will be so obliging as to help Mrs. Forbes with her work."

They left a very pink-faced baronet attached by a strand of wool to an agitated chaperon. Simon was hard put to it to restrain his mirth until the drawing-room door closed behind them.

Mimi chuckled, but then said guiltily, "I hope he doesn't make poor Mrs. Forbes too uncomfortable. I've used her badly, I fear, for she is never at ease with visitors in the best of circumstances. Now why, I wonder, is Sir Wilfred so set upon not seeing my tadpoles?"

"That's a good question. I suspect he is afraid for his dignity. He'd be bound to be noticed by your servants, and doubtless the tale would spread."

"Oh yes, he'd hate that. I really must try to get him to the scullery."

"What the devil are you about, Princess?"

She laughed merrily. "I cannot tell you."

"Then you have a purpose?"

"Now that would be telling." She pushed open the kitchen door. "Cook, we won't be disturbing you now?"

"Nay, lass, come on through. There's nowt doing in t' scullery this while." She curtsied to Simon, who smiled and nodded.

Crossing the kitchen, he noted that it was high-ceilinged, light and airy, with an impressive, new-looking closed stove. The colonel, it seemed, was as solicitous of his servants' well-being as of the plight of unknown orphans, a trait Simon appreciated after being responsible for the crew of HMS *Intrepid*. The stone-flagged scullery, with its iron pump and zinc-lined sinks, was spotlessly clean.

Mimi went straight to a Crown Derby casserole sitting on a draining board near the window. "Here they are."

"They must be the most expensively housed tadpoles in the world."

"But they don't seem very happy." She peered anxiously into the bowl. "I think those two are dead."

"Very. You need to give them clean water, I expect. See how murky it is? What do you feed them on?"

"Bread crumbs."

"Well enough, but they'd probably like a bacon rind to nibble on, maybe even some minced beef. Remember, frogs are carnivores."

"Yes, of course, I had not thought. Did you keep tadpoles when you were a boy?"

"No, I was never allowed to. I had a pet frog at school, though." Simon had forgotten Leaper, who had won several wagers for him. The memory cheered him. "He was a splendid jumper, and I was very fond of him. I was going to let him go down by the river, but he had an unfortunate encounter with a cat."

"How sad." She touched his hand in sympathy. "I don't want any more of these tadpoles to die. How shall I change the water without letting them escape?"

"Hmm, let me think. If we pour off the dirty water through a sieve, then we'll catch any that slip out."

"Do you mean to help me?"

He grinned at the mingled surprise and caution in her voice. "Don't worry, I shan't claim a reward."

A fiery blush mantled her golden cheeks—like a stormy sunset, he thought. At that moment the door to the kitchen court opened and a skinny lad in the dress of a groom appeared.

"Jacko!" She seemed delighted at the interruption.

Halting on the doorstep, the boy touched his hat. "Beg pardon, Miss Mimi, I di'n't know as you had comp'ny. I just come to take a peek at them tadpoles."

"Come in, Jacko, you can help us. This is Mr. Hurst. We're going to change their water." She explained Simon's plan.

"Right, miss. I'd best draw some water in a bucket so's we c'n fill up the dish right away." He went to the pump and started to work the handle.

"I'll ask Cook for a sieve." Mimi went into the kitchen.

Simon quickly reached into the casserole and scooped out the two dead tadpoles. The pathetic little scraps lay on his palm. "What the devil shall I do with these?" he demanded.

"Stick 'em down the drain, sir, quick afore she comes back," Jacko advised approvingly. "They'll wash down wi' the dirty water."

They exchanged a smile at their complicity in protecting the tender sensibilities of the female sex.

Mimi came back. She held the sieve over the sink while Simon carefully poured most of the water from the casserole. Two adventurous tadpoles that managed to slip out were quickly tipped back into the inch of water that remained, to join their squirming brethren. Simon set the dish down in the sink and Jacko poured in clean water from his bucket.

He poured too fast. The water sloshed over the side, taking with it three of the captives. Simon hurriedly put his hand over the drain hole and they were left high and dry in the bottom of the sink.

"You'd better rescue them," he said to Mimi, wondering whether she would actually venture to touch the tiny, twitching creatures. "Your fingers are more delicate and will do less damage."

Without the least hesitation, with the utmost gentleness, she picked them up and returned them to the casserole. "Poor little things," she said. "We must be more careful next time. I do believe they are already happier with the clean water, though." She lifted the dish out of the sink and set it on the draining board.

"They looks kind of nekkid," said Jacko doubtfully, then flushed crimson. "Beg pardon, miss, I just meant wi' all that white china round 'em."

"They need some pond weed," Simon suggested. "And that reminds me, you ought to grow some plants in that pond of yours, Miss Mimi. There was a heron down there today, and you won't have any frogs if those tadpoles don't have somewhere to hide. Have one of your gardeners take some rushes from the mere. My aunt won't mind."

"I'll do it for you, miss," Jacko assured her.

"I shall do it myself."

"Then you will doubtless need my help." Simon pretended not to notice her confusion at his provocative tone. "Tomorrow, if it is fine?"

"Tomorrow," she said decisively. "Jacko and I shall be there at nine, if you care to join us, Mr. Hurst."

"Without fail. I must leave you now, however. I abandoned my studies with Mr. Wickham to see the tadpoles, and I must return to work."

"Then you will not be riding toward the village," she said with a return to her demure manner, leading the way back through the kitchen. "I had hoped that Harriet—Miss Cooper—would visit today, but she must have been unable to escape her chores. I thought perhaps you might be passing by the vicarage and could deliver a note for me." She sighed.

Simon was instantly sure that Miss Lakshmi Lassiter had something more in mind than the simple delivery of a note, which Jacko might easily have accomplished. Intrigued, he said gallantly, "I cannot bear to disappoint you, Princess. It will take no more than a few extra minutes to ride that way."

"You are most obliging, sir." She beamed at him. "Pray come into the library while I write. I shall be brief, I promise you."

He raised his eyebrows, and she cast him a conscious look, but this time she lived up to her promise. Handing him the much-folded paper, she said, "If possible, please give it into Harriet's own hands, sir. The children—her brothers and sisters —are all too likely to forget to pass it on."

"Into her own hands," he assured her, and regretfully took his leave. He could not remember when he had been better entertained.

=== 7 ===

HARRIET SAT IN THE shabby back parlor of the vicarage with a large basket of mending at her side. Patiently she helped her little sisters darn their stockings. Mending was not an occupation she enjoyed, but teaching Sally and Prue was always a pleasure.

Perhaps, she thought sadly, she ought to give up hope of marriage and a family of her own, and try to find a position as a governess. Mimi's efforts with the tadpoles did not seem to have repelled any of her suitors more than momentarily.

"Harry! Harriet!" Jim burst into the room. "There's a gentleman at the front door asking for you."

"Who? Who is it?" She stuck her needle in the collar she was setting in a shirt for Ferdie and put it aside. "What does he want?"

"It's a stranger," said her brother importantly. "He has a letter. He wouldn't give it to me. It's got to be put into Miss Cooper's very own hands, he said."

Harriet hurried out. A strange gentleman, with a letter for her hands alone?

"He said his name is Simon Hurst," Jim yelled after her.

Her breath caught in her throat. Mr. Hurst calling on her, and insisting on seeing her in person—she had not thought he really noticed her last night, though he had sat beside her for nearly half an hour, chatting politely.

She saw his stocky frame silhouetted in the doorway.

Jim had left him standing on the doorstep, but fortunately it had stopped raining. He raised his hat as she approached with quick, light steps.

"Miss Cooper, I beg your pardon for disturbing you. Miss Lassiter instructed me to place her letter in your very hands, for fear that one of your siblings should neglect to deliver it."

He had a nice smile, she decided, taking the note, slightly disappointed that he had not come of his own accord. "Thank you, sir. Will you step in?"

"I—" His answer was cut short by an angry screech in Sally's voice.

Prue's childish treble followed. "Ooh, you're going to be in trouble, Jimmy."

"Pray excuse me, sir." Harriet sped back to the parlor.

Jim had picked up one of Sally's still-undarned stockings and, pulling on a loose thread, had unraveled several rows. Harriet promised to knit it up herself, forestalling incipient tears.

"And as for you, young man," she addressed the miscreant, "I shan't tell Papa what you did if you clean Sally's shoes for her tonight."

"But if *you're* going to mend it, I ought to clean *your* shoes."

"It was Sally you upset. Now back to the dining room with you, or I *shall* tell Papa you are neglecting your studies."

Pulling a face, Jim turned to leave. "Oh, hello, sir. Harry, here's your caller." He dashed out to rejoin his younger brother at their books.

"Mr. Hurst!" She felt her face grow hot. What must he think of her squabbling siblings?

"Forgive me, Miss Cooper. I followed to lend you my aid if necessary, but you managed admirably. As a naval officer, I couldn't have dealt better with quarreling sailors."

"You were in the navy, sir? My eldest brother, Ferdie, is a sub-lieutenant."

"What is his ship?"

"He is fourth mate on the *Bellerophon*."

They continued to talk for a few minutes, but Harriet was uneasy. She found herself in a quandary. If she asked him to be seated she ought to offer him tea, but the Coopers' one servant would not take kindly to being asked to make it in the middle of her dinner preparations. Harriet could make tea herself, but that would mean abandoning Mr. Hurst to the company of her tongue-tied sisters while she went to the kitchen.

She was glad when Prue interrupted with a timid request for Harriet to finish off a darn so that it wouldn't come undone.

"I must be on my way," said Mr. Hurst promptly. "No, I won't disturb you further, I'll see myself out. Good day, ma'am." With a nod to the children he went off.

After quickly tying off Prue's lumpy darn and starting her on another, Harriet opened Mimi's letter.

"I wish you had come Today," it began. "Mr. Hurst was Charming!!! He offered to go out of his way to carry this to you"—knowing Mimi, Harriet was fairly certain that the gentleman had been coerced in some fashion—"so I am certain he was Much Struck by you last night. I shall be at the Mere tomorrow at Nine, and he may come." At the mere at nine? What on earth was she up to now? "You must walk that way, without Fail!!!"

Mimi was determined to throw her into Mr. Hurst's arms. Folding the letter and slipping it into her pocket, Harriet made up her mind to do her best not to disappoint her friend. Though she did not find him precisely charming, Mr. Hurst was without doubt a vast improvement over Albert Pell and Sir Wilfred Marbury.

Stolen beaux or no, she thought as she set another neat stitch in Ferdie's shirt, Mimi was the best friend anyone could ask for.

Mere House glowed pinkly in the sunset. Riding homeward, Simon repeated to himself the old saw: "Red sky at night, sailors' delight." Or was it "shepherds' delight"? No matter; with any luck it meant a fine day tomorrow.

He left Intrepid in the stables and went into the house.

As he emerged from the back passage into the entrance hall, he heard Gerald's drawling voice.

"Oh no, I mean to stay with you until the end of the Season, Aunt Georgina. I have blotted my copybook in town, you see, and don't wish to face Mama's recriminations at Crossfields."

"Blotted your copybook, dear boy?" Lady Thompson's violet satin appeared in the drawing-room doorway, her head turned to address her nephew in the room beyond. "You must tell me all about it after dinner. You are not one to set tongues wagging, not like Ced— Oh, Simon! Your cousin is come."

"So I hear, Aunt."

"I daresay the pair of you have plenty to say to each other, but don't be late for dinner. I'm going up to change."

"We won't keep you from your meal," he promised, and went into the drawing room. In view of Baird's known propensity for eavesdropping, he closed it behind him. "Blotted your copybook, Gerald? I don't believe it."

"All in your service, old fellow. Good gad! What *are* you wearing?"

"I told you I wasn't bringing my new clothes. In my service? What do you mean?"

"I've avenged you, coz." Gerald dropped into a chair and lounged back, enjoying Simon's puzzlement. "I daresay you've forgot the ravishing Lady Elizabeth—the Incomparable, some call her?"

"I remember," said Simon grimly.

"The more fool you. Lady Elizabeth, having inexplicably lost the marquis's heir without a word of farewell, openly and publicly restored the handsome young viscount to her favor. Said viscount was permitted—nay, encouraged—to kiss my lady in an alcove at Almack's. To cut a short story shorter, the fair Lizzie, blushing rosily, thereupon informed me that her noble papa would be at home in the morning and would undoubtedly welcome a visit. She then proceeded to blush and whisper her way around the ballroom. Alas, for all I know Lord Prestwitton is waiting still."

"You cut and run when she was expecting an offer?"

"I did."

Simon was awed. "No wonder you don't want to face the *ton*, nor Aunt Cecilia. What can I say? You . . ."

"Spare me your thanks, old fellow. It was a novel experience, giving the biddies something to tattle about, and one should never allow oneself to become stuck in a rut, to use a distressingly rural idiom. Tell me, how do your lessons go with friend Wickham?"

"Devil take it, Gerald, the man's got me studying book-keeping!"

"Very necessary. What have you learned?"

"That the Mere House estate could make a lot more money if the rents were not ridiculously low, and that Aunt Georgina is slightly threadbare because she refuses to raise the rents. But it's *your* estate."

"It's her home. The tenants all adore her, and they plow the profits she doesn't take back into the land. Wickham makes sure it's properly done. When eventually I take over from our lady aunt—and may it be in the far distant future—this will be one of the best-kept estates in the country."

"Well, I see why you leave Wickham here rather than taking him off to Crossfields, but I hate to see the violet satin reappearing time and time again."

Gerald shuddered. "Devilish, is it not? I keep my gaze averted."

"You know what I mean."

"Possibly your untutored eye is unable to detect that there are, in fact, a number of different violet satin gowns. I know what you mean, though. You think I should insist on higher rents or make my aunt an allowance."

"It's none of my business."

"To be sure, it's not. I've tried giving her an allowance, Simon, but she simply hands out the blunt to anyone in need. Now I just make sure that Baird has sufficient to keep her in reasonable comfort and the house in reasonable repair."

"I beg your pardon. I should have guessed—"

The rattle of the door handle announced the butler. "Her ladyship," he said acidly, "prefers to dine on time."

Her ladyship's nephews headed for the stairs.

Pausing at the door of his dressing room, Gerald said in a thoughtful tone, "I wonder whether I ought to warn you . . . No, I believe the shock may be salutary."

With some misgiving, Simon continued to his own chamber. He stepped across the threshold, and a tearful voice said, "My lord . . ."

"Hush! I'm Mr. Hurst here. What the devil are you doing here, Henry?"

"I knew you couldn't manage without me, my . . . sir," said the valet passionately. "Look!" He held up a limp length of white muslin.

"My neckcloth?"

"No starch!"

"I'm much more comfortable that way. You can't stay here, Henry."

The little man wasn't listening. His appalled gaze was fixed on Simon's feet. He moaned.

Simon remembered his encounter with the mud. "You wouldn't have approved of these boots anyway," he consoled him, sitting down and beginning to pull them off. "I left my good London ones behind."

"I know, sir." Henry sank to his knees and removed the offending boots, gently but without the reverence he gave to Hoby's creations. "I packed everything up neat as could be, but Lord Litton would not allow me to bring the trunks." He regarded the boots sadly. "This type of leather simply won't take a good gloss. However, I shall naturally do my best."

"No. You can't stay. I'm just an apprentice bailiff, and I can't possibly afford a gentleman's gentleman to serve me."

"Sir, I cannot bear to see even these garments so shockingly used. Permit me to take care of your apparel and I swear I won't try to dress you, or shave you, or bring your water, or warm your bed, or even tie your cravat!"

"Oh, very well, man." Simon was touched by the fellow's loyalty. "You may stay, as long as you say you're Lord Litton's servant. I daresay no one will be excessively shocked that he needs two men to extricate him from his coat."

"I heard that." Gerald stepped into the room, discreetly closing the door behind him. "Yes, Henry, you may lay claim to be in my employ while taking care of Lord Derwent's clothes—if you can bear to have anything to do with his present attire. I wager her ladyship's footman will be overjoyed to be relieved of the awful responsibility of attempting to make my cousin appear respectable."

Although they had parted not ten minutes earlier, Gerald was already impeccably dressed for an evening in the country. He had donned pale tan pantaloons, snuff-brown waistcoat, and dark blue coat, a fresh neckcloth neatly but not elaborately tied completing the picture of elegance. It would have taken Simon, with Henry's aid, an hour or more to achieve something approaching the same effect.

Since he was not aiming at anything half so polished, another five minutes saw the cousins descending the stairs together just as the dinner gong resounded through the house. From the landing, Henry watched them. Even their movements were a study in contrasts, his master's tread resolute, vigorous, while Lord Litton bore himself with an easy grace. The valet shook his head sadly.

Lady Thompson was all agog to hear the reason for her nephew's flight from Town. To Simon's relief, Gerald made an amusing tale of it without revealing that his motive had been vengeance for the insult to his cousin. To excuse his disgraceful conduct, he simply described Lady Elizabeth's character to his aunt in the most unflattering terms.

Simon found himself wondering how the devil he could ever have thought himself in love with such a cold, calculating female.

After her ladyship retired, the gentlemen played a

game of billiards before following suit. At the bottom of the stairs Gerald decided to look in Sir Josiah's bookroom for something to read in bed.

"I'll ride with you in the morning," he proposed, turning back to the hall.

"Not unless you rise early." Simon paused on the bottom step. "I've an appointment with a young lady at nine, and I don't know how long I'll be gone."

"At nine! Young ladies never rise before noon."

"You're not in Mayfair now, coz. Here in the country, it's the early frog catches the fly."

Gerald grinned up at him. "That innocent belief just goes to prove that you haven't stayed at Crossfields since my sisters left the schoolroom. Ah well, it will take me a few days to accustom myself to country hours. I shall ride alone in the morning and see you later in the day. Good night, coz."

Taking the stairs two at a time, Simon pondered the difference between his cousin and his dead brother. Outwardly they had always appeared two of a kind, arrogant, elegant, jaded, sardonic. Yet Cedric had made Simon feel insignificant and resentful, whereas he had the liveliest affection for Gerald. Cedric's sneers had always cut him to the quick. Somehow the same insults became friendly teasing when Gerald spoke them.

Had his reactions to his elder brother been oversensitive, driven by his parents' oft-voiced opinions of their two sons? He was not much given to introspection, but he thought not. Gerald possessed two essential qualities that Cedric had lacked: a willingness to laugh at himself, and an ability to empathize.

Simon appreciated Gerald's delicacy in refraining from asking him about the lady he was meeting on the morrow. He rather suspected that his cousin would not altogether approve of the scapegrace Miss Lakshmi Lassiter.

8

MISS LAKSHMI LASSITER APPROACHED the mere with considerable trepidation. After all, the last time she had met Simon Hurst there he had been disgracefully impertinent—and she had made promises she had no intention of keeping. He had managed to inveigle a place at her dinner table, but she was determined not to grant him a dance, let alone a kiss.

Deva Lal was skittish this morning, hardly surprising in view of the clanking of the six buckets tied to the saddle of Jacko's cob, following close behind. Mimi leaned forward to stroke the mare's neck soothingly. Between the greening trees she caught sight of Mr. Hurst, alerted to their coming by the horrid noise.

Any shyness she might have felt instantly vanished. "Oh, where did you get those?" she called, her gaze fixed with open envy on his thigh boots.

"My aunt's butler found them for me." He came to meet her and walked at her stirrup back toward the water's edge.

"Baird is a dear, is he not? He found me the butterfly net, and he has lent me Sir Josiah's fishing rod. I mean to take up fishing." She announced this last with a certain defiance, but he merely nodded.

"These were Sir Josiah's fishing boots."

"I wish I could have some like them, but with these stupid skirts they would be useless anyway."

"Stupid, perhaps, but most becoming. That shade of blue suits you, Princess."

He reached up to help her down from the saddle, and for a moment his strong, warm hands clasped her waist. She was glad she had decided to wear her habit despite the encumbrance of the train, both because he admired it and because she didn't want to reveal her legs to him again. It must be the memory of riding away from him in her morning gown that made her feel hot and bothered, she decided.

All the same, the extra length of skirt was going to get in the way. "Pray turn your back, sir," she said primly. "I have brought some pins to pin up my train."

Obediently he turned away. "You need not envy the boots too much," he said, a laugh in his voice. "They make it devilish difficult to sit down, and quite impossible to ride. You should have seen me trying to mount Intrepid this morning. He looked down his nose at me as if I were a . . . frog."

Sensing a despondent tone in his pronunciation of the last word, Mimi hastened to assure him, "You cannot possibly be a frog. Frogs jump, and I don't believe you can jump an inch in those boots."

He laughed aloud. "You're probably right. I shan't try, for fear of falling flat on my face. Jacko, bring those buckets over here. There are some rushes growing in shallow water, and a patch of cress. I brought a spade and fork."

"That's well thought on, sir." The groom clanked after him. "There weren't nowhere to tie 'em on to poor ole Brownie alongside these pails, but I borried a trowel from Mr. Renfrew, as is our gardener at the Hall. He'll have me guts for garters ifn I don't take it back safe and sound."

Her skirt securely pinned—she hoped—Mimi hurried after them. Despite her good intentions, she was soon damp and muddy, her hair falling in wisps over her face. She was enjoying herself too much to care. Taking off her hat, she tossed it to the ground.

Jacko, soaked to the knees, carried a bucket full of fresh green rushes out of the mere. Mimi took it from him.

"It's not too heavy. I'll carry it over to Brownie."

She turned to find a gentleman riding toward her along the bank. As he neared, she recognized Viscount Litton and saw his satirical look change to surprise.

"Miss Lassiter, is it not?" He raised his glossy beaver and bowed.

Mimi curtsied, feeling foolish. "How do you do, my lord."

"I thought I recognized the bay. . . . Good gad, Simon, it *is* you. I'd no idea you had an interest in cottage industries. Basket weaving, I take it?"

"If we were going to make baskets," Mimi pointed out, "we would not need the roots, so we could just cut the rushes instead of digging them up."

"Of course. How slow-witted I am at this hour of the morning," he said politely. Too politely—Mimi was sure he was mocking her. "I assume, then, that you have some other purpose in mind?"

"To plant them elsewhere, obviously," came Simon's voice from behind her. "You certainly are obtuse this morning, Gerald."

Mimi glanced back at him. Still standing in the mere, he was grinning at the viscount, not in the least discomfited by his lordship's irony. Nor did Lord Litton appear to resent the insult. She recalled that, whatever the difference in station, they were connected through the Thompsons: Lord Litton was Sir Josiah's nephew and Mr. Hurst was related to Lady Thompson. They seemed to know each other well.

"Ah, not cottage industries but gardening," said the viscount. "I never suspected you of such versatility."

"A bailiff must turn his hand to many tasks. Here, Jacko, take this pail of flags. They'll be blooming soon, but I hope they won't mind being transplanted. That's the last, is it not?"

"Aye, sir, they'm all full."

Recalling her bucket of rushes, Mimi picked it up. Lord

Litton promptly swung down from his horse and tied it to the nearest tree, saying, "Allow me to be of assistance, ma'am."

She looked dubiously at his spotless buckskins, gleaming top boots with snowy white tops, and superbly tailored jacket. Even dressed for riding he cast Sir Wilfred's finest finery in the shade. It would be almost indecent to let him carry anything so commonplace as a bucket.

"I'm stuck," said Simon.

Mimi and the viscount swung round. From the bank, Jacko reached for Simon's hand and tugged. Simon wavered wildly and nearly sat down. Mimi giggled.

Lord Litton sighed. "Pray excuse me, Miss Lassiter." He went over to the edge of the mere and reached for Simon's other hand.

Mimi was laughing so hard that she didn't notice Harriet's approach until little Prue piped up, "Harry, that's the gentleman who called on you yesterday."

"Harriet, I'm glad you came. Mr. Hurst has been so very helpful and now the poor man is stuck in the mud. Oh, they've pulled him out."

As Simon emerged glugging from the mere, Jacko staggered backward and landed on his rear end. With a neat bit of footwork that would have drawn praise in Gentleman Jackson's Boxing Saloon, Lord Litton kept his balance. Leaving Simon breathing heavily on the brink, he joined the ladies. His boots still gleamed, and not a fold of his cravat nor a hair on his dark head was out of place.

He looked on Harriet, fresh and neat in pale yellow muslin, with unmistakable approval and, Mimi thought, with some uncertainty.

"I believe you have met Miss Cooper, my lord."

"Ah, yes, our worthy vicar's daughter." He smiled as Harriet curtsied. "I think you and I are the only sane people in this Bedlam, Miss Cooper. These must be your sisters?"

"Sarah and Prudence, my lord," Harriet told him shyly.

The little girls curtsied. Prue, at six years old, had not quite mastered the art and she wobbled. The viscount put out a hand to steady her. She beamed at him.

"I'm getting better," she assured him. "We're going for a walk. Do you want to come?"

To Mimi's astonishment the top-o'-the-trees nobleman, after a moment of grave consideration, said that that was a delightful idea and offered Harriet his arm. As they strolled away, the children running ahead, she stared after them, then glanced disconsolately down at her soiled riding habit.

Oh well, all in a good cause, she thought, shrugging her shoulders. It was a pity, though, that Harriet had not had a chance to talk to Mr. Hurst.

"Do you mean to help us, Princess?"

Simon and Jacko were tying the buckets full of plants to the patient Brownie's saddle. Mimi picked up her hat and went to join them.

"Thank you, sir, we should never have managed without you." She held out her hand to Simon.

He took it, but replied, "We're not finished yet. There's the planting to be done."

"Oh, but I didn't expect . . ." she began, disconcerted.

"I never leave a task unfinished. Let us be on our way before those clouds I see in the west arrive."

To ride when he was walking would have been rude, she felt, even though he looked more like a laborer than a bailiff with the fork and spade over his shoulder. Leading Deva Lal, she fell into step beside him.

"You did a splendid job of pinning up your train," he congratulated her with a grin. "I quite thought I was going to have to leave Sir Josiah's boots behind me in the lake."

Suddenly the day was sparkling again. She laughed. "You looked so very funny. That was further proof that you're not a frog, whatever your horse may think. Whoever heard of a frog getting stuck in a pond?"

"I can't be a sailor anymore, and I'll never make a town beau," Simon pointed out to Gerald that evening as they sipped Sir Josiah's ruby port. "I might as well make the best of it and accustom myself to rustic pursuits."

"I am acquainted with a number of gentlemen who enjoy the pursuit of rustic beauties," his cousin drawled, "but devil if I know any who pursue them through knee-deep mud."

"I've no intention of pursuing Miss Lassiter, I assure you." To himself, he qualified that statement: *Except to gain my promised rewards.* "I'm damned if I know how she inveigled me into this morning's escapade."

"I have met Miss Lassiter before," Gerald mused, holding his glass up to the light and admiring the rich color. "I thought her a well-behaved, insipid miss no different from a hundred of her kind. How wrong I was! To what do we owe the transformation, I wonder?"

"I don't know, but I'm quite certain there's method to her madness. She's more or less admitted to some deep-laid plan, to what end I've no notion."

"One shudders to think. Pray do not allow yourself to be ensnared by the tiresome child."

"I'm in no danger—she thinks me a bailiff. But what of you and Miss Cooper, coz? I near fell back in the lake when I saw you walking off with her on your arm as if you were strolling in Hyde Park with a blue-blooded debutante."

"With a blue-blooded debutante, as you vulgarly put it, or even with Miss Lassiter, I might indeed arouse expectations. The daughter of a country parson has more sense than to let her hopes be raised."

"You mean no more than a flirtation, then?" Simon hoped he didn't sound disapproving. He rather liked Harriet Cooper and would be sorry to see her hurt.

"Gad no," said Gerald, bored. "Miss Cooper has not a flirtatious bone in her undeniably shapely body. We spoke of parish business. Shall we join Aunt Georgina?"

Simon drank down the remains of his glass of port and followed the viscount from the dining room.

Gerald paused with his hand on the drawing-room door handle. "Besides," he said with a lurking smile, "we were very thoroughly chaperoned by Miss Sally and Miss Prue."

* * *

The clouds Simon had seen blowing up passed over after dropping a few showers. The next day the sun shone once again. Mimi wanted to talk to Harriet, privately, without Mrs. Forbes or Mrs. Cooper or the children. She sent Jacko to the vicarage to see if Harriet could escape for a while and meet her in the gazebo at the top of the ha-ha.

"Miss says her mum's much better and she'll be there at midday," the groom reported.

"Good. I can go and inspect the plants in the pond while I'm there, to see if they have survived transplanting. Thank you, Jacko."

Shortly before noon, Mimi walked down through the gardens, abloom now with peonies, tulips, and pansies. She particularly liked the pansies, with their cheeky faces raised to the sun. Picking a few, she pinned them to the bodice of her apple green walking dress. Mrs. Forbes was right; a lady should always carry a few spare pins.

When she reached the top of the ha-ha, Harriet was already coming up the steps. They went together into the gazebo, a small open summerhouse decorated with lacy, white-painted fretwork. More than anything else in England, it reminded Mimi of India, of the cool pavilions in the gardens of her grandfather's palace. For a moment she was overcome with nostalgia for the fierce old man, for fountains and still pools with pale-pink lotus blossoms floating, for the sound of bare feet on marble floors and soft voices murmuring in Hindi, for odors of incense and spice.

She shook away the memories. This was home now, the fresh fragrance of lilac breaking into bloom nearby, the green, fertile farmland stretching into the distance, and the church bells in the village striking twelve.

"How pretty you looked yesterday," she said, taking a seat on the cushioned bench beside her friend. "Yellow suits you. You must have that gown I wore at dinner the other day. I don't know why I didn't think of it before."

"Oh, I couldn't."

"You must. I look a fright in it, and as long as it's hanging in my wardrobe I shall be tempted to wear it to see if it's really as bad as I think it is. How annoying it was of Lord Litton yesterday to take you away before you could speak to Simon."

"Simon?"

"That's what Lord Litton calls Mr. Hurst, and Lady Thompson too, and after hearing them, that's how I think of him. It's a nice name, isn't it? Don't worry, I wouldn't address him by it to his face. Or maybe I would," she added darkly. "He calls me Princess when we're alone."

"Alone!"

"With no one around but Jacko. What do you think of him?"

"Of Jacko, Mr. Hurst, or Lord Litton?" asked Harriet, laughing.

"Of Mr. Hurst, of course. It doesn't matter what you think of the other two."

"He seems a pleasant, well-spoken gentleman. I have not seen enough of him to know more."

"Did he not stay and talk to you when he brought the note? I sent him specially."

"Yes, we talked for a while, about the navy."

"The navy! How on earth did you come to mention that Ferdie is in the navy?"

"It was Mr. Hurst who raised the subject. He used to be a naval officer."

"I wonder why he left? I should think that would suit him much better than estate management. He's nicer than Sir Wilfred and Albert Pell and the others, don't you think?"

"Oh, yes, he is much more sensible."

"And amiable," said Mimi firmly. "How *very* annoying of Lord Litton to come along just then and drag you off like that."

"He did not precisely drag me away. It was Prue, rather, who dragged him. I was surprised at how kind he was to the children. I always found him rather daunting before."

"Well, no matter. He's a viscount. It's Simon Hurst we must concentrate our efforts on, though I daresay we had best not give up on the others quite yet. I wonder if he likes music? You have such a lovely voice, Harriet. I shall give a musical evening."

Harriet chuckled. "That is particularly noble of you, when I know how you hate sitting through Sophia's endless performances upon the harpsichord."

"All in a good cause. Besides, it will be the perfect occasion for an idea I have to offend the others."

"What are you going to do?"

"Nothing too shocking, but it's a secret. In the meantime, I'm going to ask Albert Pell to teach me to fish. That should upset him, don't you think? He is always fulminating against females getting in the way on the hunting field."

"Yes, and Sir Wilfred will consider it unfeminine, besides risking untold damage to your attire."

"It's a pity he didn't see me yesterday," said Mimi, giggling. "Lord Litton stared at me with such haughty disapproval I wanted to— Oh, look! They are coming!"

She jumped up and ran to the top of the steps, followed at a more dignified pace by Harriet. Two horsemen had just entered the paddock through the gate that led toward Mere House. Mimi waved and started down the steps.

She reached the bottom just as the riders trotted up.

"Well met, Miss Lassiter, Miss Cooper," cried Simon, while his lordship doffed his hat and bowed. "I persuaded Gerald to ride this way so that I could inspect yesterday's handiwork."

"I am on the same errand," said Mimi, smiling up at him, then turning with a slight curtsy to the viscount. "Good day, my lord."

"How do you do, Miss Lassiter. I own myself all agog to discover the progress of your cottage industry. Your servant, Miss Cooper." He bowed again, but remained mounted when Simon swung down from the saddle.

"Shall I hold your horse, sir," Harriet offered, "while you and Mimi look at your plants?"

"I'll take Intrepid's reins," said his lordship quickly. "While not the most fiery of steeds, he is too large for you, ma'am."

Simon handed him the reins, and he and Mimi moved closer to the pond.

"The reeds and rushes look quite happy," said Mimi. "And see over there—two yellow flags in bloom already. Are they not pretty?"

"I'm afraid the watercress has wilted. It was difficult to avoid breaking the stems."

"Perhaps it will put up new shoots. Harriet's mama says you sometimes can't say for several days, or even weeks, if a new plant will take. Look, the tadpoles are all clustered around the reeds. You were right, they like them."

"That reminds me. I brought Sir Josiah's butterfly net and stopped by the mere, much to Gerald's disgust, to fish out some pondweed for the casseroled tadpoles. We forgot to get any yesterday. The net's stuck through my stirrup leather, much to Intrepid's disgust. I hope the weed didn't fall out."

They returned to the horses, where Lord Litton had dismounted and was chatting with Harriet. Simon produced several long, dripping strands of greenery from the net.

"You cannot carry that, Mimi," Harriet protested. "You will ruin your dress."

Mimi had no particular fondness for that dress and would have taken the pondweed anyway, but Simon held it away from her.

"So you will. I'll ride up to the Hall with it."

"All right. I'll meet you in the scullery in ten minutes. Harriet, my lord, will you come and have some luncheon?"

"I must be going home," said Harriet regretfully. "I promised Mama not to be away too long."

"Then pray allow me to escort you, Miss Cooper," Lord Litton requested. "I had in any case intended to pay my devoirs to the vicar today."

So they parted. Hurrying up the steps and across the

gardens, Mimi realized remorsefully that despite her best intentions she was monopolizing Simon while poor Harriet was left with the disdainful viscount. She hoped Harriet recognized that it was no use setting her cap at his lordship; toplofty noblemen of his ilk simply didn't go about marrying the daughters of impecunious country parsons.

At least, she was fairly sure they didn't. But what had he meant by paying his "devoirs" to the vicar?

When Simon reached the scullery, Mimi was already there, peering into the casserole. She looked up as he deposited the butterfly net in the nearest sink.

"What does 'devoir' mean?" she asked him without ceremony.

"Devoir?" He was startled, having forgotten his cousin's use of the word. "It's a French word meaning to have to, to be obliged to. Did you never learn any French?"

"No, but I speak Hindi and some Urdu, and I can read a little Arabic. That doesn't make sense. Lord Litton said he was going to pay his devoirs to Mr. Cooper."

"Oh, that's an English phrase meaning to pay his respects. The living of Salters Green is in Gerald's gift now, I imagine, since Sir Josiah's demise."

"Then shouldn't Mr. Cooper pay his respects to Lord Litton?"

"There are those who would expect it, certainly."

"Oh." She frowned in thought, biting her lower lip, her little teeth gleaming white against her dark skin. "Perhaps Lord Litton is not as disagreeable as I thought."

"He's not such a bad fellow when you get to know him," Simon told her, hiding a smile.

She dismissed the subject, turning back to the tadpoles. "We had best change the water before we put the pondweed in. I have the sieve. Cook wouldn't take it back after it had 'them nasty slimy creatures' in it."

"All right. I'll draw some water first."

"I can call Jacko to do it."

"That's all right, Princess. I'm not such a useless fribble I can't pump water."

"You're not a fribble at all. Harriet says you used to be a naval officer." She sounded accusing.

"I was," he admitted, remembering too late that Aunt Georgina had advised him to conceal the fact.

"Why did you leave the navy?"

"My brother died, and my parents wanted me at home."

"Oh, I'm so sorry." With instant sympathy she laid her hand on his arm. "How sad to lose your brother and your profession at once. That must be why you are learning estate management. I hope you will like it and not miss the sea too much."

"Less and less," he assured her, and realized that it was true.

=== 9 ===

"IT'S UTTERLY INFURIATING," SAID Mimi. "Albert Pell was positively enthusiastic when I asked him to teach me to fish."

With Jacko's help, Harriet mounted Shridatta and settled herself in the sidesaddle. They rode toward the village.

"Papa says it's because the Pells' farms are in shocking condition," Mimi continued. "Albert will endure even a female indulging in sporting pursuits for the sake of my fortune."

"Your father told you that!"

"Why, yes. He would not stop me marrying anyone I truly loved, but he cannot approve of Albert Pell, nor of Sir Wilfred."

"My father would prefer to see me wed to Mr. Lloyd or Mr. Blake," Harriet admitted. "Though they are both of lower station in the eyes of the world. He says they are both respectable and well-intentioned. But oh, Mimi, Mr. Blake is so dry, and I cannot like Mr. Lloyd. He is not at all what I believe a clergyman ought to be."

"That's because no one can measure up to your papa. Mr. Lloyd talks about religion a great deal, but it is Mr. Cooper who . . . who makes one want to become a better person."

"I begin to think I shall never marry," said Harriet dolefully. "Maria was so very fortunate to meet Mr. Talmadge at the Chester assembly."

"If your sister was lucky enough to meet a pleasant and eligible gentleman, there's no reason you should not be too. It's less than a month until the next June ball. I must say it's a pity, though, that you're disillusioned with our local beaux. I see what it is: the company of Mr. Hurst and Lord Litton has spoiled you."

"Oh no, I hope not!"

"Mr. Hurst is more agreeable than any of them," Mimi pointed out, "while the viscount's elegance puts Sir Wilfred's foppery to shame and his manner is not near as obnoxious as Albert's."

"You are unfair. Lord Litton's manners are excellent, not merely superior to Mr. Pell's."

"It's not easy to be fair when someone looks at you as if you were a frog who has just jumped out of his salad."

The thoughtful look in Mimi's eye made Harriet decidedly uneasy. "Mimi, you would not!"

"Well, no. There's no reason to drive the viscount away, for he does not admire me in the least."

"And he would never think of me as an eligible bride anyway."

"I'm afraid not. I *wish* I could give you half my fortune, Harriet! But as I cannot, I had better persevere with my plot, just in case you don't meet anyone suitable at the assembly and Mr. Hurst doesn't come up to scratch. Oh, here we are at Mullins's already. You won't mind waiting while I choose some ribbons?"

They dismounted in the middle of the row of whitewashed shops with their Welsh slate roofs and crooked black beams. Leaving Jacko standing by the bow window with the horses, the girls stepped down into the tiny, low-ceilinged room where Mrs. Mullins sold ribbons and buttons, needles and knotting-shuttles, thread lace and handkerchiefs.

Mimi was at once absorbed in discussion with the proprietress, while Harriet passed the time of day with an elderly parishioner who had dropped in for a chat.

The church clock struck the quarter.

"Mimi, you have an appointment."

"Oh, yes, though it will not hurt to keep him waiting. Which of these ribbons do you prefer, Harriet?"

"The russet satin, but that poppy-red velvet will suit you better."

"I'll take five yards of each, Mrs. Mullins, and wrap them separately, if you please." While the parcels were tied with string, she peered out through the distorting panes of the bow window at the village green opposite. "Drat, there's Sir Wilfred, and he's seen Jacko. Never mind, he can ride with us to the mere and then escort you home."

She took the packages with a word of thanks and they went out into the street, blinking in the sunshine after the gloom of the shop.

"Good day, Miss Lassiter." Sir Wilfred swept off his curly-brimmed hat and bowed. "Buying yourself some pretty fripperies, eh?" He nodded carelessly to Harriet. "Miss Cooper."

"We are going to the mere to meet Mr. Pell and catch some fish," Mimi told him.

"Fish!" At that moment the baronet looked rather like a fish himself, his eyes popping and his mouth round with surprise. "Oh, ha ha, you mean you're going to watch Pell fishing."

"*I* am going to catch fish. I hope," she added.

"Oh . . . ah . . . I . . . er . . . how . . . er . . . interesting. You too, Miss Harriet?"

"I am just riding with Mimi, sir."

Sir Wilfred sighed with relief. "Didn't suppose for a moment . . . Allow me to help you mount, Miss Harriet."

Mimi cast a triumphant glance at Harriet and saw an answering twinkle in her friend's eye. She was feeling pleased with herself as they rode down the village street toward the mere. Sir Wilfred might be a popinjay but he was the wealthiest of her four suitors, able to keep Harriet in comfort if only he could be persuaded to offer for her.

Albert Pell was waiting impatiently on the flat stone bridge over the stream that fed the mere. He strode to meet them and helped Mimi dismount while Jacko unloaded Sir Josiah's tackle from Brownie's back. Harriet and Sir Wilfred seated themselves on a nearby wooden bench, but Mimi, disappointed, noted that they seemed to have nothing to say to each other. Instead, they both watched her with obvious anxiety.

Albert's scorn was equally obvious as he inspected Sir Josiah's rod, though he didn't comment. Indeed, beside his own it looked sadly primitive, eight feet or so of split cane to his twelve, and a reel mounted on a wooden pin rather than metal. Mimi didn't care.

"Show me," she demanded.

"First you bait your hook. I brought some worms."

"You mean you stick the hook through the worm?"

" 'Sright. Feeling squeamish?" He laughed, looking smug in his masculine superiority to such feminine sentimentality. "Here, I'll do it for you."

"No, I won't use a worm. I brought some bacon rinds. If the tadpoles like them, the fish will too."

He shrugged. "You won't get a bite, but if that's what you want."

They each baited their own hooks, then Albert demonstrated a cast. Mimi watched carefully as his rod whipped back, then forward, and the cork float flew out over the still water of the mere and dropped to the surface. She raised Sir Josiah's rod to try it, then decided that her hat and gloves were in the way. Setting the rod down, she took them off and dropped them beside her.

"Miss Lassiter!" Sir Wilfred started up in dismay. Harriet pulled him down again.

Mimi picked up the rod. With Albert's critical gaze upon her, she whipped the tip backward, then jerked it toward the water.

"You've hooked me, dammit!" roared Albert. Dropping his own rod, he stretched his arm back over his shoulder in vain. The hook had caught his coat neatly in the very center of his back, where he couldn't reach it from either above or below.

Mimi giggled.

"Careful, you'll tear your coat," called Sir Wilfred.

In his efforts to get at the hook, Albert started stamping about on the bridge. One large foot demolished the cork crown of Mimi's hat, snapping its curling ostrich plume.

"No, really, I say!" Horrified by the wholesale destruction, Sir Wilfred rushed up onto the bridge.

Mimi was laughing too hard to be of much assistance. "K-keep still, or we c-can't help you," she gasped, grabbing Albert's nearest arm.

Sir Wilfred extricated the hook, then sadly picked up Mimi's hat and tried to restore it to something resembling headware.

"See what I can do," he muttered with a hopeless air, and carried it back toward the bench.

Mimi saw that while she had been blinded by tears of laughter, Lord Litton and Mr. Hurst had ridden up. Of course they knew she would be fishing today, as Lady Thompson's permission had been sought. Still on horseback, they were watching with identical grins. She waved to them.

Swinging round, Albert snarled, "Damme if we'll catch a minnow with all these people around. I might 'a' known it was a mistake to take a female fishing."

Ignoring him, Mimi cast again.

"Not like that," snorted Albert.

But this time her float sailed out over the water and came to rest just where she had aimed it. It bobbed gently, then sank. She felt a tug on the line.

"I've caught something!"

In an instant Albert's arms closed about her. There was nothing loverlike in his embrace; his entire attention and energy were on her bending rod and the spot where the float had disappeared into the water. Cursing steadily only half under his breath, he played the fish with the skill of a born sportsman and gradually drew it toward them.

It was at least three feet long and incredibly ugly, a dark, mottled gray with a narrow, protruding lower jaw, viciously toothed. As it thrashed on the surface, a burst of applause came from the bank.

"A granddaddy pike! Hold it still a moment and I'll gaff it," Albert ordered.

"No!"

"What d'you mean, no? The line'll break if I try to land it with the rod."

"I mean let it go. You can't kill it." Somehow the pike's sheer ugliness spoke to Mimi's heart. "Take the hook out of its mouth and let it go."

"If you don't want it, I'll take it. Pike's good eating."

"It's mine. I caught it. I want to let it go," she insisted.

With an unbelieving glower, Albert took a knife from his pocket, leaned over the low parapet of the bridge, and cut the line a foot above the fish's head. It sank without trace.

"I said to take the hook out!"

"You saw those teeth!"

They glared at each other, then beyond him she caught sight of Mr. Hurst sitting on the bench beside Harriet, talking to her. An overwhelming urge to join them seized Mimi. She turned to stalk past Albert, forgetting the length of the rod in her hand. It whacked him across the chest and broke in two.

Whether she had deprived him of breath or just of words, she couldn't guess. Purple in the face, jaw clenched, he picked up his tackle and strode silently past her to fling himself astride his huge roan stallion and gallop away.

Sir Wilfred hurried toward her, her mangled hat in his hand. "Better than nothing," he assured her. "Just wear it till you get home."

Taking it from him, she looked at it with disfavor but set it on her head, the plume dangling down her cheek. As he bent to retrieve her boot-trodden gloves, she heard Lord Litton's languid voice.

"I must admit it was a better comedy than any farce I've ever seen at the Haymarket."

Harriet and Simon Hurst laughed. Hurt, Mimi felt for a moment like an outsider, the object of their mockery. Then Jacko came up, grinning.

"Cor, miss, you put Squire's son in a right passion," he congratulated her.

Mimi recalled her purpose. "Yes, I did," she said with a satisfied smile. Fishing for fish was much more effective than fishing for tadpoles, though she was sorry the poor pike had a sore mouth. She took her besmirched gloves from Sir Wilfred, and they went to join the others.

"You beat Pell at his own game," Simon greeted her. "No wonder he's unhappy."

"I wish I had wagered on your success, Miss Lassiter," said the viscount. "I have been after that brute this age."

"But I am glad you let him go," put in Harriet.

Lord Litton smiled at her. "Yes, for it gives me another chance."

Mimi heaved a happy sigh. "It was all very exciting. I'll ride back to the vicarage with you, Harriet."

"Can't go near the village in that hat," begged Sir Wilfred.

She took it off and regarded it thoughtfully. "No, you're quite right, sir. I'll go without it." With a sweeping gesture, she tossed it into the mere.

Gently it bobbed on the ripples, the broken feather trailing in the water. Then it jerked and suddenly submerged.

"I do believe your pike has taken his revenge," said Simon.

He was expected by Mr. Wickham and had to take his leave, but the other two gentlemen escorted Mimi and Harriet back toward the village. Sir Wilfred, casting many an uneasy glance at Mimi's bare head, rode determinedly as far from her as he could, leading the way with Harriet.

Politeness forced the viscount to stay at Mimi's side. She was still annoyed with him for his remark about the Haymarket farce, and she was astonished when he said with apparent sincerity, "May I have your permission to try again for the pike, Miss Lassiter?"

"But it is not my lake, my lord. You must ask Lady Thompson."

"Not your lake, certainly, but the fish, I feel, is your protégé. I have no desire to cause any distress."

"Oh no, I simply did not wish to be responsible for his death at Mr. Pell's hands."

"I quite understand. However, the brute wreaks havoc among the other fish in the mere. It even eats frogs, you know, in which I believe you take a particular interest."

"Then you may catch him with my blessing!"

"May I ask what bait you used with such success?"

Mimi flushed. "Mr. Pell was sadly shocked, I fear, but I simply could not let him stick the hook through a live, wriggling worm. I used a bacon rind."

Lord Litton shouted with laughter, making Harriet and Sir Wilfred turn around to stare. "That is what I shall try, then," he said, "unless I can persuade my aunt to give up a feather from one of her bonnets. Incidentally, it was a pleasure to watch you rout Pell, Miss Lassiter."

Perhaps he had been mocking Albert, not her, she thought. Perhaps Simon was right and his lordship was not as supercilious as he had seemed.

When they reached the vicarage, she decided to go in to see Mrs. Cooper. Lord Litton had business in the village, and Sir Wilfred hurriedly and unconvincingly excused himself for the same reason. Harriet looked disappointed.

"Sir Wilfred was afraid that if he came in he would have to escort me home hatless," Mimi consoled her as they went up the path. "Here, this is for you." She thrust into her friend's hands one of the packages she had purchased earlier. Through the hole she had poked to see which ribbon it contained, a bit of russet satin protruded.

"Oh, Mimi, I cannot accept it."

"You must. It won't suit me in the least, and I can't return it, for Mrs. Mullins needs the money. It will be perfect for retrimming the primrose gown to wear at my musical evening. You must look your best. Albert Pell and Sir Wilfred are already vexed with me, and that evening I intend to upset Mr. Lloyd and Mr. Blake."

Her glee was infectious. Opening the front door, Harriet couldn't help smiling at her despite her doubts, and assuring her, "I simply cannot wait to find out what you are planning for your musical evening!"

===10===

SIMON WAS LOOKING FORWARD to the Lassiters' musical evening with no ordinary degree of anticipation.

Gerald was not. "I am forced to attend a horrifying number of such events in town," he said in his most bored voice as they went in to dinner the day before. "You will make my excuses, Aunt Georgina."

"Indeed I shall not! It would be unpardonably ill-mannered of you to cry off, and if there is anything to be said for you, Gerald, it is that your manners are generally impeccable."

"I thank you for that encomium, Aunt." Bowing, he seated her, and he and Simon took their places.

"I know that as a connoisseur you abhor being subjected to amateur musicians," said Simon, "especially screeching sopranos—"

"Of which there are many professionals," his cousin admitted.

"—but however tedious the music, no affair hosted by Miss Lassiter is likely to prove dull."

Baird, ladling soup, was heard to choke. His mistress fixed him with a steely glare.

"True," said Gerald dryly. He sighed. "Very well, I shall attend."

"What instrument does Miss Lassiter play, Aunt?" Simon inquired.

But Lady Thompson could not recall ever having heard Mimi play, nor sing. "I expect she has arranged the occasion to allow Harriet to shine," she said. "Harriet's voice is charming, and dear Mimi is very fond of her."

Gerald muttered that if he had a guinea for every debutante whose voice had been described as charming, he would be rich as Golden Ball.

Despite his reluctance, the party from Mere House were the first guests to arrive at Salters Hall. Waring ushered them into the drawing room. Following his aunt and cousin, Simon heard her surprised exclamation, heard the tone of deep amusement in Gerald's "How do you do, Miss Lassiter." And then Mimi was before him.

Hands palm to palm, she bowed her head and murmured, *"Namaste."*

She was wearing a speedwell blue sari with a broad, patterned border of cloth of gold. At her throat gleamed a collar of gold set with sapphires. A diaphanous veil sprigged with gold embroidery covered her hair and draped her slender arms and shoulders, almost hiding the sapphires at her ears. As she raised her head, Simon saw that in the center of her forehead, above black eyes sparkling with mischief, she had painted a round black mark, signifying, he recalled, that she was unwed.

"Namaste," he responded gravely, pressing his palms together and bowing his head.

"Oh!" She clapped her hands in delight. "How did you know what it means?"

"I don't precisely. Just a greeting and a blessing, isn't it? But my ship was stationed at Bombay for six months, and I went ashore every chance I had."

"No wonder you talked sensibly about India when you came to dinner. Excuse me, Si— sir, here come the Marburys."

Instead of moving on to speak to the colonel and Mrs. Forbes, Simon lingered to see the effect of Mimi's costume on the would-be-fashionable Marburys.

The ladies met the challenge with a glassy stare and a stiff "How do you do," before passing Simon with a negligent nod to emphasize his low status. Miss Marbury whispered audibly to her mother, "All that gold—so gaudy."

"Positively vulgar," Lady Marbury snorted. "Good evening, Lady Thompson. It is such a relief always to know what you will be wearing."

Simon didn't listen to his aunt's riposte to this doubly barbed remark. He was concentrating on not laughing at Sir Wilfred's expression. The baronet, unable to drag his gaze from Mimi's black-marked forehead, appeared to be both startled and a trifle envious.

"Daresay you will set a new fashion, Miss Lassiter. Much easier for a female to set a new fashion," he added discontentedly. "Of course, painting the face was modish for both ladies and gentlemen thirty years ago, and the placing of patches was an art. Little scope for imagination in a gentleman's dress these days."

"True, a modern gentleman's attire is monstrous dull," said Mimi, blithely ignoring Sir Wilfred's pink, purple, and lime green floral waistcoat.

Disconsolate, he turned away as Waring announced the Coopers. Simon would have liked to see what the vicar and his family—Harriet's younger sister had been invited, too—thought of Mimi's transformation, but it was past time he spoke to his host.

The colonel was watching his daughter with a fond smile. "What think you of my naughty baggage, Mr. Hurst?" he inquired.

"That she is as audacious as she is beautiful, sir."

"Her beauty reminds me of her mother, but my poor Prithivi never had a hundredth of Mimi's spirit."

"If she has set the cat among the pigeons, she has done so with all due deliberation and for her own purpose."

"Aye, you can be sure of that." Colonel Lassiter chuckled, but then turned serious. "However, she don't always foresee the unintended consequences of her scheming. It's a comfort to me that Harriet Cooper is her friend. She's a sensible girl, but not always able to curb Mimi's starts."

As the colonel turned to greet Mr. and Mrs. Cooper, Simon was sure that he had been tacitly asked for his help in protecting Mimi from the untoward results of her actions. Flattered as he was by the request, it left him feeling a trifle uneasy. Why had the colonel chosen *him* to confide in?

He found himself beside Sir Wilfred, who said to him in a low voice, "Splendid notion, that veil. Great help in hiding a flawed complexion."

Simon drew himself up and replied with a haughty disdain worthy of Gerald, "I was not aware of any flaws in Miss Lassiter's complexion."

"No, no, of course not," stammered the baronet. "Speaking generally, don't you know. Any number of ladies ought to wear a veil." He suddenly recalled some urgent message to be delivered to his mother, and took himself off.

Harriet Cooper joined Simon. "I could not help overhearing you just now, sir," she said. "It was splendid of you to come to Mimi's defense."

"I doubt she would thank me, ma'am. She believes herself capable of fighting all her own battles, I suspect."

"Oh yes, and other people's too. For the most part she is right, for she is as dauntless as she is kind and generous. But though Mrs. Forbes has been with her for several years, and she has been in England for over a year now, I sometimes wonder if she quite understands English Society."

"You're thinking of her dress tonight?"

"Oh no, that is a deliberate effort to . . . well, it is deliberate, I assure you, and odd but unexceptionable. No, I was thinking how utterly undisturbed she was when . . ." Harriet flushed slightly, ". . . when Mr. Pell put his arms around her by the mere the other day."

Simon laughed. "I never thought of that. The battle with the fish absorbed my attention, I suppose."

Her blush deepened. "I assure you, sir, I should have been quite overset by such . . . by such . . ."

". . . an embrace," he finished for her. "Yes, I do see what you mean. But after all, she had her revenge, first by releasing the fish, and then by breaking her rod over him."

Gerald had come up in time to hear his last words. "I gather the Pells are not to join us tonight," he said, "whether taking fright at an evening of culture, or still piqued by the pike, I cannot guess. I have just made the acquaintance of your sister Judith, Miss Cooper. You and she are to sing a duet, I collect?"

They embarked on a conversation about music which quickly took Simon out of his depth. He looked around the room, noting that Mr. Blake and the Reverend Lloyd had arrived, but his mind was on Harriet's disclosure of her feelings about Mimi. He couldn't believe the vicar's daughter was in league with the colonel to involve him, yet the effect was the same: both had confided their misgivings in such a way as to amount to a silent plea to him to help.

He must be looking particularly trustworthy tonight, he thought wryly. Perhaps it was the combination of a superior valet with inferior clothes. He could blame it all on Henry.

Waring approached with a tray of glasses. Simon took one and looked around the room again as he sipped a fine Madeira.

Mimi was talking to Judith Cooper, a plump, bashful-looking blonde a few years younger than Harriet. Judith shook her head vigorously, yellow ringlets flying, and Mimi went to consult Mrs. Forbes. She moved with a fluid grace that reminded Simon of Gerald. She had the carriage of a princess, but her escapades scarce fitted her to be a viscountess. Gerald had referred to her as a tiresome child, Simon recalled.

He had a feeling that her Indian costume was not the only surprise she had in store for this evening.

At that moment she clapped her hands. "Everyone is here. If you will all find yourselves seats, I shall ask Sophia to begin our concert."

Miss Marbury swept forward to take her place at the harpsichord, clearly accepting this invitation as her due. "I shall play a suite by Couperin," she announced.

Simon sat down on a blue brocade sofa against the

wall, and Mimi, having seen the rest of her guests seated, came to join him. The metallic tinkle of the harpsichord began.

And went on, and on, and on. Simon shifted restlessly.

Mimi caught his eye. "I'm sorry," she whispered. "I wanted to start with Harriet and Judith singing a nice short duet, but Judith was too shy. Do you dislike music?"

"Not in general," he whispered back, "but I confess to preferring the pianoforte to the harpsichord."

"So do I. Mrs. Forbes wanted to buy one, but Papa said that as I do not play, a harpsichord would take up less space. I believe he regrets it."

Simon glanced at the colonel's grimly patient expression and grinned. Gerald looked as if he might expire from boredom at any moment. In fact, of all the audience only the performer's mama and Mr. Blake the lawyer appeared entranced.

"Blake seems to be enjoying it," he pointed out *sotto voce.*

"He told me that 'Baroque music most perfectly encapsulates the laws of musical composition,' whatever that means. He says, 'Music is the highest art and unsurpassed pinnacle of expression of Western civilization.' "

It was difficult to tell when she spoke in an undertone, but Simon gained the impression that there was a certain scorn in Mimi's voice.

Lady Marbury's glare silenced them both. Fortunately, the Couperin suite ended soon after. Before Sophia could launch into an encore scarcely justified by the unenthusiastic applause, Mimi jumped up and asked Harriet and Judith to sing.

The sisters came forward hand in hand, one in pale yellow and one in pink. Beside Mimi, they looked very English with their fair hair and rosy cheeks. At least that was how they struck Simon, a world traveler familiar with all the varied races of mankind. To others, he realized as he noted one or two unguarded expressions, they simply made Mimi look more foreign.

Was that what she wanted, or was it one of the undesired and undesirable consequences her father and her friend had spoken of?

She was smiling as she returned to his side. "This will be much nicer," she assured him.

The unaccompanied English folk songs were indeed charming. They sang "The Ash Grove" and "Come You Not from Newcastle," Judith in a rather breathless contralto, Harriet's voice a pure and true soprano. Remembering Gerald's scorn for amateur singers, Simon glanced at his cousin, to find him looking interested for the first time that evening.

After the two songs, Judith retired to her father's side and Mrs. Cooper sat down at the harpsichord. Simon groaned softly. Mimi frowned at him.

"This won't be at all like Sophia's," she hissed. "I've heard Harriet practicing."

Simon had to agree with her when Harriet's voice joined her mother's accompaniment in the glorious strains of Mozart's "Exultate, Jubilate." Gerald actually sat up straight, as if he was afraid to miss a note, and at the end the applause was lengthy and heartfelt. Mr. Blake called for an encore.

Harriet, blushing with pleasure, curtsied deeply and then held up her hand for silence. "Thank you all, but I shall not sing an encore. It is Mimi's turn now."

As Mimi stood up, a footman placed a large embroidered cushion on the floor in front of the harpsichord. There was a murmur of curiosity from the audience. Then the butler appeared with a long, narrow, many-stringed instrument borne carefully in both hands. Mimi knelt on the cushion, and he handed it to her. It had a round sound box at one end, and a fretted neck that reached a foot or two above her head. Recognizing it, Simon racked his brain for the name.

The limpid, mellow tones as she tuned it reminded him: it was a sitar.

"I shall play an evening *raga*," Mimi said, a faraway look in her eyes. "It is based on a song about the love of the god Krishna for the milkmaid Radha."

Simon heard a hiss of indrawn breath and saw Mr. Lloyd lean toward Mr. Cooper, his round face red with indignation. His lips formed the words "heathen immorality." Mr. Cooper shook his head.

Mimi's slender brown fingers rippled across the strings, calling forth a strange series of notes, an incomplete, unfamiliar scale. Mr. Blake, proponent of music as the pinnacle of Western civilization, frowned. Simon was sure he had already decided that Eastern music was by definition primitive. He was not going to make any effort to understand an idiom unknown to him.

Gerald, on the other hand, looked fascinated. Simon glanced around the rest of the audience, but already the shivering harmonies and complex rhythms were pulling him back in memory to sultry evenings spent wandering through the streets of Bombay. The lure of the mysterious East was strong in him. He should never have left the navy while there was so much of the world yet to be seen.

The last notes faded into silence. The listeners stirred uncertainly, applauded still more uncertainly. Simon went to help Mimi to her feet.

"That was too short," he said.

She smiled. "After all, my purpose was to startle, not to bore them."

Gerald came up to examine the sitar. He asked some technical question about the number of strings.

"I don't know, my lord," Mimi confessed. "I just play it as a young English lady plays the harp or harpsichord, without any claim to true virtuosity."

"Then I shall never know which of the sounds you produced were intentional and which accidental. Nonetheless, it was an interesting experience."

"It sounded authentic to me," Simon said.

"I defer to your expertise," Gerald assured him ironically.

Waring announced that a buffet supper was served in the dining room, and the guests made their way thither. Simon was not in the least surprised when the aroma of a score of spices met his nostrils. His mouth watered.

"Biriani, korma, pulao, bhaji, paratha," he recited. "Now there no expertise is needed. I'll eat whatever's put before me."

"Not a great variety," said Mimi regretfully. "Mrs. Forbes had one or two receipts, and my maid recalled a few more. But I cannot vouch for their authenticity either, since I couldn't find all the right spices even in Chester. Besides, Cook was in high fidgets at being asked to make them. There are a number of English dishes, too, for the less adventurous."

The three of them were last to reach the dining room, just in time to hear Sophia Marbury's disapproving voice.

"Just a roll and butter, thank you. I do not care to . . . Why, Mama, how odd! Someone has decorated the table with cow parsley."

"Queen Anne's lace," corrected Mrs. Forbes anxiously.

"And pot marigolds," Lady Marbury pointed out to her daughter. "Extraordinary!"

"Calendulas," chorused Mrs. Cooper and Lady Thompson.

Mimi threw them a grateful glance, but Simon could tell she was hiding a smile. "In the holy city of Benares," she announced, "devout pilgrims float garlands of marigolds down the sacred River Ganges in honor of the gods."

"Pagan superstition!" Shocked, Mr. Lloyd turned to Harriet and offered to serve her from the vast array of dishes on the sideboard.

"An original bouquet," said Gerald dryly.

Simon caught Mimi's eye. It must have been the spirit of mischief there that prompted him to ask, "And the cow parsley?"

"Why, Mr. Hurst, I thought you knew," she said. "In India, cows are sacred, too."

=11=

"AND MR. LLOYD TOLD me much might be forgiven anyone brought up in such unfortunate circumstances," said Mimi indignantly, closing her dripping umbrella and dropping it in the umbrella stand. "So I described the splendors of my grandfather's palace in glorious detail."

" 'Unfortunate' is scarcely the word," Harriet agreed. "Come into the parlor. Mama is teaching the girls in the dining room. What was Mr. Lloyd's reaction to that?"

"His little eyes glistened with greed and he said he meant unfortunate in a spiritual sense. If I would only allow him to guide me, he was sure he could persuade me of the superiority of the Church of England over the benighted idolatry of Hinduism."

"I daresay he would say the same if you were a Papist. Papa believes all faiths are worthy of respect."

"I'm sorry, Harriet, I did think my Indian evening was bound to drive both him and Mr. Blake into your arms," Mimi said, plumping down into the sagging seat of an aged armchair. "And with any luck Sir Wilfred, too, but he actually admired my sari. You're not mending again! I can't darn, or mend tears. Give me something easy to do, like a split seam."

"Are you sure?" Harriet sorted through the overflowing basket and produced a small pink garment. "Here is a pinafore of Sally's. She burst the seam, so it is to be handed on to Prue. Poor Prue! The youngest never has any new clothes."

"I know *you* are still wearing out Maria's petticoats though she has been married three years."

"No, Judith is tall enough at last! I shall have a new petticoat for the Chester assembly. Sir Wilfred may have admired your sari, but he also told me my gown was exceedingly becoming."

"I knew those ribbons would be perfect for it. You can't wear that to the ball, though. Just let me think." Her needle slowed to a halt as she mentally searched her wardrobe.

"I shall wear the pink tamboured muslin I inherited from Maria," Harriet said firmly, and changed the subject. "Your Indian evening was by no means a failure. Mr. Blake called yesterday."

"He did? Splendid! Tell me all about it."

"He complimented my singing, and then explained in excessive detail just how Indian music fails to follow the laws of musical composition. I told him I expect they have their own laws, and he was quite put out of countenance."

"He came up to the Hall, too. He stayed fifteen minutes and thanked us for an interesting evening. He managed to avoid the word 'music' the entire time. Lord Litton, on the other hand, asked me to play the sitar again for him some time. Mr. Hurst was with him—he helped me change the tadpoles' water. They said they were on their way to the vicarage when they left. Did you see them?"

"Yes. His lordship had business with Papa, but afterward he sat with Mama and me for at least a quarter of an hour. He is amazingly approachable for a nobleman. I wish . . ." She sighed and left the thought unfinished. "He was most civil."

"And Mr. Hurst?"

"He is truly amiable, as you said. Mama and Papa like him too. I believe I should like to be married to him."

Mimi quashed the unpleasant sinking feeling in her middle and said briskly, "Then I must try harder to bring it about. The trouble is, none of the efforts I have made to upset the others seem to disturb him in the least.

Perhaps I shall think of something to do at Lady Thompson's picnic. Have you received your invitation yet?"

"It came this morning. She has invited all the children, is that not kind? I do hope the weather will improve."

They both stared hopefully at the window, but the unrelenting drizzle continued to stream down the panes.

When Mimi took her leave an hour later, it was still raining. As she retrieved her umbrella, Harriet said, "You did not walk here alone, did you?"

"It seemed silly for Jacko or Asota to get wet as well as me. Papa took the carriage to Highbury to look at the manor, because he just received Lord Daumier's approval. I don't mind walking in the rain." Seeing a protest forming on Harriet's lips, she added hastily, "You simply cannot wear pink to the assembly, you know. Sophia's gown will be pink."

"I know, pale-pink crêpe lisse with rose ruching, over a white satin petticoat embroidered with rosettes of seed pearls. But . . ."

"Leave it to me," Mimi commanded, and set off down the garden path.

A gusty breeze had come up, and by the time she reached home she was damp despite the umbrella. The Indian climate definitely had its advantages, she thought. At least it only rained during the monsoon season; at other times of year, one could safely set a date for a picnic far in advance.

Weeks might pass before the English weather would permit Lady Thompson's picnic! Still, there was no harm in planning ahead. As Asota helped her take off her damp pelisse, Mimi decided to call on her ladyship on the morrow to see if she had any good ideas.

After several days of rain, at last the sun shone again. Mimi was on tenterhooks when Lady Thompson insisted on allowing two days to pass for the ground to dry out somewhat, but the warm, still days persisted. At noon on the third, a varied collection of carriages, riders, and walkers converged on the mere.

On the bank near the old jetty, the Mere House servants had spread rugs and cushions, with small tables and chairs in the dappled shade of new-leafed trees for the older guests. A long trestle table bore cold chicken and ham, a huge wheel of crumbly orange Cheshire cheese, pies and cakes, wine, lemonade and cider, bowls of wrinkled russet apples.

As her father handed Mimi out of the barouche, however, her gaze was on the mere. There, tied to the jetty, floated a small, flat-bottomed skiff, just as Lady Thompson had promised. Since Sir Josiah's demise, it had lain unused in a boathouse hidden by bushes at the far side of the mere. The estate carpenter, Knowles, had rescued and refurbished it. Fresh varnish gleamed in the sun, the oars were neatly shipped, and plump blue cushions graced the benches.

No one else seemed to have noticed the little boat, not even young Jim and Peter Cooper, who had found a dish of jam tarts and were quietly gobbling them.

Today was to be Harriet's day. If Simon Hurst persisted in paying more attention to Mimi than to her friend, she was going to go boating without him.

He was approaching now, with his aunt and cousin, to greet them. Lady Thompson bore off Mrs. Forbes to seat her at a table. Lord Litton stood chatting to the colonel.

"Miss Cooper is saving you a cushion and a patch of rug," Simon said to Mimi. "She is afraid Miss Marbury will arrive and . . . er . . . impose her presence, I collect."

"I expect sitting on the ground is too undignified for Sophia. And for Lord Litton, surely. Now I come to think of it, they would suit each other very well. I'm surprised she does not set her cap at him, for his is the only title in the neighborhood and Sophia is determined to catch a title."

"Gerald told me he was vigorously pursued a couple of years past, when she first came out. I understand he was forced to make his feelings brutally plain."

"No wonder she avoids him, then. I expect he was

perfectly odious to the poor girl. To be sure, why should he settle for a baronet's daughter when I'm sure any number of titled ladies would be glad to wed him."

"Any number," Simon agreed, grinning. "You won't repeat the tale, will you, Princess? I ought not to have told you."

"No, you ought not, and your punishment is at hand. Here come the Marburys. Lady Thompson and Lord Litton are otherwise occupied, so you will have to play host." She laughed at his groan. "I shall join Harriet," she said, departing.

Harriet waved from a rug near the trestle table, where Judith was scolding her brothers, caught jam-handed. Mr. Lloyd was sitting beside Harriet, his uneasy look suggesting that either he or his dignity was suffering some discomfort. He attempted to stand as Mimi approached.

"Pray do not rise, sir," she said, dropping gracefully to a cushion next to him. "Only those who are accustomed to sitting on the floor can manage it without clumsiness. In India, only Europeans use chairs. My grandfather, the Rajah, sits on a large cushion, and even the gods and the Buddha are generally depicted seated in the *padmasana*."

The parson's face turned an interesting shade of purple.

"What is *padmasana*?" asked Harriet quickly.

"*Padma* is the lotus, and *sana* simply means position. It's a *Yoga* posture, sitting cross-legged with each foot resting on the opposite thigh. I could show you if I was wearing a sari." Mimi tried not to giggle—Harriet was pink-faced now, obviously wishing she hadn't asked. "There's Albert Pell," she said, to give them both time to recover. "I'll ask him to join us."

The squire's son was staring longingly at the laden table, not quite ill-mannered enough to follow the Cooper boys' example in starting to eat before everyone was assembled.

"Veal-and-ham pie," he greeted Mimi. "Our cook can't make pastry worth a damn."

"I'll see that there is a pie next time you dine at the Hall," Mimi promised.

"Rabbit pie's the best. I'll bring you round a brace next time I go shooting."

"Fish pie is good too," Mimi said.

Albert guffawed. "First catch your pike, damme. I've brought my rod and Litton says I can have a go at the old devil this afternoon."

"I wish him luck. Will you come and sit with us, sir?"

But he refused to leave his post by the food, as if he were afraid the veal-and-ham pie would disappear the moment he turned his back. Mimi needed another gentleman for this phase of her plan, but Mr. Blake had not come and Sir Wilfred was monopolized by a visiting friend of Lady Marbury's. There were one or two other unmarried gentlemen present, sons of acquaintances of Lady Thompson, but she didn't know them well enough to invite them to join her. She returned to Harriet, who had soothed Mr. Lloyd back to his usual pink complexion.

Sitting down again, Mimi listened impatiently for some minutes to a discourse on the superiority of monotheism, addressed to Harriet but directed at her. She was about to ask a question about the Holy Trinity when Simon came up to them.

"Miss Cooper, Miss Lassiter, may I fetch you some luncheon?"

"Thank you, sir." Harriet smiled up at him. She looked very pretty in a walking dress of blue-sprigged muslin, Mimi thought. "That would be kind in you, especially after Mimi has informed us that anyone not bred to it is bound to be clumsy rising from the ground."

"I was bred to it," said Mimi, jumping up. "I prefer to choose my own, thank you, Mr. Hurst."

"I tried to persuade Aunt Georgina to provide a curry," he said as they moved to the table, "but she said that her cook is overset if asked to make a French sauce and might drop dead if asked for Indian fare."

"Oh dear, that would never do." Mimi chuckled. "Papa decided that after a year of nothing but English food he wants a curry now and then, and our cook has been muttering dire warnings ever since. Sally, can I help you reach something?"

"Yes, please, Miss Mimi," said the little girl. "I can't pour the lemonade."

"Thank you, Miss Mimi." Judith looked flustered. "I said I'd help her when Prue has hers, but she won't wait."

"You have your brothers to watch, too, do you not? I'll give you a hand."

Everything was working out splendidly. Mr. Hurst, though his manners were less polished than Lord Litton's, was by far too polite to abandon Harriet after filling a plate for her. Mimi went to sit with Judith and the children, helping to cut up ham, spread bread with butter, wipe sticky fingers, and stop Jimmy and Peter from throwing apple cores at each other.

When she glanced over at the group she had left, she saw that Harriet and Simon were talking companionably. Much to her surprise, Lord Litton had joined them. As she watched, he picked up Harriet's glass and rose with indubitable grace to go to the table to refill it. Though he had been sitting on the rug, his coat was unwrinkled, his hair smooth. It was unnatural, Mimi felt, knowing the back of her skirt was most certainly creased.

Simon looked round, caught her eye, and smiled. His sandy hair was ruffled and his neckcloth had nearly untied itself. He looked comfortable. She smiled back.

Everyone else finished eating, even Albert Pell. Baird and a couple of footmen, having discreetly left the gentry to enjoy their picnic, had returned to clear up the gentry's mess, but Prudence was still struggling with an apple. She was determined to eat it, although she had a wobbly tooth which she was equally determined not to lose just yet. The boys raced off, and Sally was anxious to follow them.

"I'll go with her, Judith," Mimi offered. "Slice the apple thin, and when Prue has eaten it come after us."

She took Sally's hand, and they set out through the trees. Jim and Peter had found a climbable silver birch and were halfway up it.

"I want to climb too," said Sally.

"You're too little," shouted Peter.

"I'm only a year younger than you."

"You're a girl," Jimmy retorted.

That was enough to decide Mimi in favor of Sally, but she could not allow it without consulting Judith. She looked back the way they had come. Judith and little Prue were quite close already—and not far behind them strolled Harriet, Simon, and Lord Litton.

"Drat!" muttered Mimi. They were bound to ask her to walk with them. She would accept if she thought she could detach the viscount, but she didn't know enough about Indian music to interest him, and he scorned everything else she did. Better that Harriet should have both gentlemen than that Simon's attention should be distracted from her. "Go and ask Judith if you can climb," she said to Sally.

As the child ran to meet her sister, Mimi slipped away through the trees and hurried down to the mere.

"Miss Lassiter can't have seen us coming," said Simon. "She's probably gone to look for us—or for you, at least, Miss Cooper. We'd best go after her."

His words went unheeded. Sally had noted Harriet's approach and wanted Judith overruled.

"She says I mustn't climb with Jimmy and Peter! Pray say I may, Harriet."

"Oh dear, you had better not, love. If you got stuck, neither Judith nor I might be able to help you."

"If that is your only concern, Miss Cooper," Gerald said, "I shall pledge to go to the rescue."

Harriet beamed at him. "How kind, my lord."

"But what about Mim . . . Miss Lassiter?" said Simon to their retreating backs.

Giving up, he went after her himself. When he reached the picnic ground, he found that most members of the party had either gone for a stroll or were in a decidedly somnolent condition. Mimi was nowhere to be seen.

Simon remembered that Albert Pell had intended to fish for the giant pike. Perhaps she had joined him. There he was, on the bridge over the stream, but still no sign of . . .

What the devil did Miss Lakshmi Lassiter think she was doing all alone in a boat in the middle of the mere?

All alone in a boat in the middle of the mere and bailing desperately with her inadequate little hands.

"Devil take her," he muttered, sprinting down to the jetty. By the time he reached it he had his coat off—and the boat was visibly sinking beneath her. Dropping his coat, he ran to the end of the jetty and pulled off his boots. When he glanced up again, Mimi was floundering in the water.

He dived in and swam toward her, his heart pounding furiously, threatening to choke him. Surely she couldn't drown in an ornamental lake on a summer's day, within a hundred yards of a picnic party!

Raising his head to check direction and distance, he found himself face-to-face with Mimi.

Intent on her dog paddle, she flashed him a small smile before once more concentrating fiercely on swimming. Amused, angry, admiring, above all relieved, he swam beside her to the jetty.

Reaching up, she started to pull herself out of the water. The thin muslin of her gown clung to her shoulders, her arms, her—

"Stop!" he ordered grimly. Startled, she obeyed. With one heave he hauled himself onto the jetty. On the bank a semicircle of spectators moved closer. In front of them, the colonel and Baird reached the landward end of the jetty. "She's fine, sir," Simon called. "Baird, her ladyship's shawl."

The colonel nodded, his thin face losing its anxiety, while the elderly butler hurried off. Simon turned. Mimi was once again attempting to pull herself out.

"Help me!" she demanded, indignant.

"Stay there."

"But it's cold!"

"I said stay there." He went to get his coat from the colonel, who had picked it up.

"Need a hand, my boy?"

"No, sir, I'll manage it. I'm wet already."

"Then I'll see if I can disperse the audience." They grinned at each other.

Simon went back to Mimi. "Can you hold on with one hand while you slip the other arm into my coat?" he asked.

"It will get wet. Why won't you help me out first?"

"Because everyone is watching, and they will be shocked if you expose yourself to their gaze in your present condition."

"Oh. All right, I'll try, but I'm cold and I'm getting a bit tired."

She raised one arm, revealing the curve of her breast clearly outlined by the wet fabric. Simon knelt down, trying to keep his eyes from the lovely sight while inserting her arm into the sleeve of his coat. Both proved difficult.

"My hand is slipping. I can't hold on much longer."

"This isn't going to work." He tossed the coat behind him and she gripped the edge of the jetty with her freed hand.

"Simon, I want to get out," she wailed.

Throwing discretion to the winds, he reached down and helped her scramble up onto the worn gray wood. For a moment she was kneeling clasped to his chest, her eyes a few inches from his. He read apprehension in their dark depths, remembered his demand for a kiss, cursed himself silently as he released her and grabbed his coat.

"There's something down my bodice, wriggling about."

Simon closed his eyes as Mimi, wriggling like whatever it was she had caught, plunged her hand down the front of her dress. He couldn't decide whether to pray that she would manage to get it out, or that she would need help.

"I have it. A tadpole, wouldn't you know it? Poor little thing. Back you go into the water."

He opened his eyes. She was smiling uncertainly at something behind him. Glancing back, he saw that Baird was standing there, imperturbable, with Lady Thompson's paisley wool shawl spread between outstretched hands, shielding them from view. The butler's gaze was fixed discreetly on the middle distance.

"Her ladyship sleeps on, sir," he reported.

Mimi giggled, shivering. Simon quickly helped her into his coat and buttoned it. As they stood up, Baird handed over the shawl and turned his back. Somehow Simon managed to tie the shawl about Mimi's waist as a skirt without yielding to the temptation to run his hands down her slim hips. He, too, was shivering now, not only from the cold. He pulled on his boots over dripping breeches. This was becoming a habit!

"Come on." He took her hand. "The sooner we get you home, the better."

"I venture to suggest, sir, that Mere House is a trifle closer than Salters Hall."

"Good thinking, Baird. Come with us and make us each one of your hot lemon-and-honey concoctions."

Though Colonel Lassiter had dispersed the crowd, Simon was very much aware as they hurried to Lady Thompson's landau that everyone was watching. His exasperation with Mimi's idiotic solo voyage returned. Why was the silly chit so determined to ignore the proprieties, not to mention her own safety?

With a groom and Baird perched up in front, it was impossible to ask her on the short drive, and the moment they set foot in Mere House Lady Thompson's housekeeper swept her away. Grumpily, Simon submitted to Henry's scolding ministrations.

Back at the mere, Lady Thompson awoke feeling chilly. Lady Marbury informed her with great relish that her butler had appropriated her shawl, and regaled her with the story of Miss Lassiter's scandalous misdeeds.

On the bridge, Albert Pell hooked a floating cushion. The blue cover burst as he disentangled it from his line, filling the air with feathers that drifted gently down to bob on the water's surface. A huge pike rose to investigate. It gave the angler a knowing look, and with a flick of its powerful tail shot away.

Albert Pell swore loud and long.

=12=

"IT WOULD APPEAR, MY lord," said Baird, taking Gerald's hat and gloves, "that young Knowles, a cautious sort of chap where his own skin is concerned, failed to determine whether the craft was capable of supporting the weight of a person. If it floats, it floats, he reckoned."

"Thank you, Baird. I shall speak to Knowles. Is my cousin come down yet?"

"In the drawing room, my lord. Her ladyship is above stairs with Miss Lassiter."

"Poor Aunt Georgina. A dramatic end to her picnic!" He suddenly grinned at the butler. "I understand you were of material assistance to Simon?"

"I did my poor best, my lord." He bowed as a gold coin changed hands. "Perhaps you might suggest to Mr. Hurst, my lord, that if he intends to make a habit of swimming in the mere, he might enjoy it more if he dressed more suitably."

"Henry's having fits, is he? Gad, I wish I had seen it," said Gerald, and headed for the drawing room.

As he entered the room, Simon saluted him with his glass of hot lemon-and-honey-and-rum. "Splendid fellow, Baird," he observed.

"He seems to think you would enjoy swimming more if you did not always go in fully clothed."

"So he has already told me. There's nothing mealymouthed about the man. I'll try to remember next time."

"I regret having missed the drama." Gerald sighed.

"You're jealous, coz, because you would have been quite useless as a rescuer."

"On the contrary, I can swim quite as well as you."

"Better, but it would have taken you half an hour to remove your coat and boots!"

"True, alas. It is a lowering reflection that all I am fit for is rescuing little girls from trees."

"Is that what you've been doing all this time? You don't look like it."

Gerald glanced down with a modicum of satisfaction at his still-impeccable attire. "Miss Sally Cooper was halfway up a silver birch when she realized she had overestimated her climbing ability," he explained. "A charming family, the Coopers. Do I dare inquire as to why the indomitable Miss Lassiter took the boat out alone?"

"Damned if I know," said Simon.

"But Mimi, I do not understand *why* you went rowing alone yesterday," said Harriet.

"I saw you coming, and I thought that if I was not with you Simon's attention would be concentrated on you. How was I to guess he'd follow me?"

"How very fortunate that he did!"

"Fustian! He didn't rescue me, I swam to shore by myself." Her indignation revived. "And then he made me stay dangling in the water for ages. I nearly froze!"

Mimi shivered at the memory of his arms about her, pressing her to his chest. His sea-colored eyes, so close to hers, had flooded her with a swift tide of warmth that as swiftly ebbed, leaving her heart fluttering in tremulous agitation.

"I think I achieved my purpose," she said uncertainly. "He didn't say a word all the way to Mere House."

"Whyever not?"

"He was angry with me. Because he got wet again, I suppose. I don't want to dance with him at the assembly!"

"It would be shockingly discourteous to refuse him if he asks," Harriet pointed out. "Unless, of course, your card is already full."

"That's a stupid rule. Why should I have to dance with someone . . . Unless my card is full? That's it. I shall make sure I'm engaged beforehand for every dance."

As the day of the Chester assembly approached, Mimi began to feel panic-stricken. If Simon won his dance, he'd have two out of three of the rewards she had foolishly promised, and what was to stop him from taking the third?

Being Mimi, however, she was not about to tamely await his triumph. When Mr. Blake called at Salters Hall with some legal papers for the colonel, she exerted all her charm.

"I am sadly nervous about the assembly," she told him, her black eyes wide and wistful. "As you know, we came to Cheshire too late to attend last year. Suppose no one asks me to stand up? How horrid to be a wallflower!"

"Ahem. There is small chance of that, I vow, Miss Lassiter. However, if it will ease your mind, allow me to engage you in advance for a country dance."

"Oh, sir, that is excessively kind of you." She batted her eyelashes.

"And a quadrille?" In his excitement at this unwonted encouragement, the lawyer forgot his usual cautious cough before he spoke. "I trust you know the rules of the quadrille, ma'am?" He laughed dryly to show he was joking."

"Certainly, but I shall ask Mrs. Forbes to remind me once more of the figures. I know how important rules are to you, sir."

Similar tactics met with similar success when Sir Wilfred, Albert Pell, and the Reverend Lloyd came to call. Still more satisfactory was that each gentleman in turn then called at the vicarage and asked Harriet to stand up with them.

"It's a sort of insurance, I wager," Mimi told her friend as they waited for Jacko to open the gate to the paddock. "In case I do anything shocking, they hope to retrieve their dignities by dancing with someone utterly respectable. Can you come up to the hall tomorrow afternoon? Asota should have finished making your gown by then."

"Mimi, I told you I cannot accept—"

"Fustian. Your mama has nobly offered to chaperon me, since Mrs. Forbes doesn't wish to go. Besides, I mean to look my best, and how vain I shall appear if my best friend is less finely dressed. Think how everyone will stare when we enter the ballroom arm in arm."

Harriet smiled. "Your arguments are most convincing. How can I possibly risk making you appear vain? Yes, I can come to the hall tomorrow."

"Good. Sophia is going to regret wearing insipid pink. Thank you, Jacko."

The groom grinned at her as they rode through into the paddock.

"Are you engaged for every set already?" Harriet asked. "I have two or three left."

"That's all right—you *do* want to dance with Simon, and you must keep one free in case you meet an eligible stranger as Maria did. Papa wants my first dance, and I'm sure he will take the last one if necessary. Now I'd like to see how my tadpoles are doing, if you don't mind waiting a moment."

She rode to the pond and dismounted, letting Deva Lal wander off to crop the grass with a nearby pair of horses. After a week of fine weather, the ground was firm even right on the bank. The little willow had put forth leaves of tender green; the rushes she and Simon planted had flourished, and the yellow flags were in full bloom. He had seemed so easygoing then. What a pity he had turned out to be so dictatorial, she thought.

The train of her habit over her arm, Mimi crouched and peered into the water. "They are growing fat," she called to Harriet. "Near as big as the ones in the casserole. I believe they will soon start to grow legs."

"Ugh!" said Harriet.

"Here come my lord Litton, miss," Jacko announced.

Turning her head, Mimi saw the viscount and his mount sail over the gate. He rode with the same easy mastery he brought to everything he did. As he cantered toward them, she eyed him speculatively.

She had not intended to attempt to wheedle him into requesting a dance. He had by far too knowing a look to be taken in by the stratagem she had used on the others. But she was afraid Simon would never believe that her father would not give up a dance to him. Standing up, she returned the viscount's greeting. At least she could introduce the subject of the ball and see where it led.

"Good day, my lord. We are on our way to Mere House to see Lady Thompson. She has offered to lend Harriet a fan for the assembly."

Harriet looked at her in astonishment and swallowed a protest. It was the first she'd heard of borrowing a fan. "Her ladyship is most kind," she murmured.

"My aunt is a generous soul. Are you looking forward to the ball?"

"Oh yes," said Harriet.

"Especially as both our cards are nearly full already," Mimi added. "It is a great occasion for us, though I daresay a country assembly means nothing to you, accustomed as you are to frequenting the grand affairs in London." There, she had cornered him. He could scarcely agree without appearing odiously conceited.

He cast a mocking glance at her, and she knew he had seen through her ploy. However, he turned back to Harriet and said, "On the contrary, I was greatly looking forward to the assembly, until I heard the alarming news that your card is all but full, Miss Cooper. Dare I hope that you will promise me a dance before it is too late?"

Harriet blushed. "I shall be most happy to do so, my lord." Perhaps her hands tightened on the reins, for Shridatta sidled nervously. At once Lord Litton leaned down from his saddle and seized the mare's reins. Harriet's color deepened. "Thank you, sir."

He smiled at her. "I believe I was too hasty. You are too good a horsewoman to lose control."

"Shridatta is a true lady," said Harriet, bowing her head and stroking her mount's neck soothingly.

"Like her rider."

Mimi was worried. When he chose, Lord Litton could

be as charming as he was handsome, but she wished he would not choose to exercise his charm on Harriet. If Harriet were to fall in love with him, it could only lead to heartbreak.

"Deva Lal is very biddable too," she said, to attract his attention. She looked around, to find that her mare had wandered off to the far side of the field. "Oh, *drat*! I wish I had taught her to come when she's called."

"As biddable as her rider," said his lordship, laughing. "Shall I fetch her for you, Miss Lassiter?"

"I'll go, m'lord," Jacko offered. "She'm a mite headstrong at times. Likely she'll try to dodge your lordship, being as she don't know you." He and Brownie went after her.

"A mite headstrong, eh?" The viscount was doing a poor job of repressing his mirth.

Hands on hips, Mimi glared up at him. If it wasn't for the necessity of avoiding Simon, she wouldn't dance with Lord Litton if he were the last man on earth. Of course, he hadn't asked her yet.

Before she could decide whether to give him a setdown or try a little cajolery, he had once more turned to Harriet. He told her he was on his way to see the vicar about a Mere House tenant whose wife was ill.

"Aunt Georgina has seen to it that the family has all the creature comforts," he said, "but I am hoping that Mr. Cooper will be able to suggest some village woman who could go in to help them."

Harriet knew just the right person, directed him to her cottage, and offered to check on his tenant daily to see that all went well.

"She is a parishioner, so it is one of the duties of a vicar's daughter," she assured him.

"Or of a landlord's . . ." His words were lost as Jacko trotted up leading Deva Lal.

Lord Litton at once dismounted to lift Mimi into the saddle, then mounted again and took his leave. He started toward Salters Green and they turned toward Mere House.

"Oh, by the way, Miss Lassiter," he called after them, "I trust you, too, have a dance to spare for me?"

"Better than that, my lord; I shall be most happy to spare you two." Mimi rode on, grinning, before he could answer. Revenge was sweet.

"But you said you only had one free," Harriet pointed out, shaking her head at her friend's boldness.

"Mr. Blake will have to give up his quadrille. I never told him I'd dance it with him, only that I knew the figures—the rules, as he called them. I'm surprised he didn't call them laws."

Appealed to to cover Mimi's story, Lady Thompson recalled a fan of silver lace she had carried in her youth. Her butler, to no one's surprise, knew in exactly which trunk in the attic it had been put away. To the ladies' dismay, age had tarnished it completely black.

"I shall clean it, my lady," Baird promised. "After all," he added caustically, "one of the most important duties of a butler is taking care of the silver."

"Then you shall spruce up my moonstone necklace, too," her ladyship retorted. "It is set in silver, my dears, and will be quite perfect with Harriet's gown as you have described it. I simply cannot wait to see the pair of you."

=13=

IT WAS FORTUNATE INDEED that Lady Thompson simply couldn't wait to see Mimi and Harriet in their ball gowns, for Simon insisted on arriving in Chester a good half hour before the assembly began.

He explained to his cousin as the carriage carried them toward the city. "I know you think she was lying when she said—"

"My dear fellow!" Gerald interrupted, shocked. "I would never accuse a lady of lying. *Prevaricating* is the word I used."

"—when she said their cards were nearly full, but suppose she meant it? She owes me a dance, and I'm determined to stand up with her tonight."

Lady Thompson fanned the flames. "Recalling the difficulty you had in dining with the Lassiters, Simon, I suspect Mimi may have deliberately filled her card beforehand."

"She's quite capable of it," he admitted. "But I did sit down to dinner at her side, remember. I mean to stay one jump ahead of her even if I have to pay the musicians to play an extra set."

"As a frog, you should have no difficulty staying one jump ahead," murmured Gerald. "What a pity the saltarello is no longer fashionable."

"The saltarello? I don't recall a dance of that name," said Lady Thompson, puzzled.

"You are by far too young, Aunt Georgina. It was popular, I believe, in the sixteenth century. It involved a good deal of leaping and hopping." He sighed at the thought. "An undignified age."

"You'd have looked elegant in doublet and hose," said Simon, "and I'd have been strangled by the ruff."

He looked down in some dissatisfaction at his evening clothes. His dove-colored pantaloons were spotless, his dancing shoes as glossy as Henry could make them, his coat the correct shade of blue. But they were all old and worn—almost as outdated as the saltarello. As soon as his masquerade was over, he would buy new clothes. There must be some middle ground between fashionable discomfort and shabby comfort.

Aunt Georgina had said that Mimi was going to dress up in all her finery. No wonder she wanted to avoid dancing with him.

When they reached the Derby Arms, he combed his sandy hair into compliance, then stared long and hard at his cravat in a looking glass. He had allowed Henry to tie it for him, in the style known as the Oriental, and he willed it not to wilt.

He went through to the ballroom. Gerald was talking to a local landowner, and Aunt Georgina had found a pair of old acquaintances to gossip with. Simon's arrival went unnoticed. He joined a group of young men already waiting near the door to spot likely-looking partners to whom they could beg an introduction of the master of ceremonies. And the young ladies started to drift in— pink, pale blue, primrose, lilac, and white, plump and skinny, pretty and plain.

The Marburys arrived. Dutiful if unenthusiastic, Simon asked Sophia for a country dance. Condescending, she deigned to grant him one despite his lowly status. He prayed as he signed her card that he hadn't picked the one set Mimi still had free.

He was bowing his thanks when Colonel Lassiter and Mrs. Cooper entered. They stepped aside to give their names to the master of ceremonies. Framed in the double doorway, each with her arm about the other's waist, stood an ethereal vision in silver and white and a dazzling figure in scarlet and gold.

Simon stared. Mimi's fiery silk gown, embroidered in gold thread, opened over a petticoat of cloth of gold. At her throat, wrists, and ears carnelians gleamed, and gold was woven into the black braids piled on her proudly held head. She was magnificent, every inch a princess.

Simon realized that everyone else was staring too. All conversation at that end of the room had ceased.

He stepped forward, grinning as he noted Mimi's pleased smile and Harriet's blush. Their finery had no more changed them than his had changed him, despite Gerald's and Henry's efforts in town.

"Spectacular!" Simon assured the young ladies. "The effect is all you could possibly have hoped for, Princess. But I trust you don't mean to remain inseparable all evening. Miss Cooper, pray say you will stand up with me."

"I shall be delighted, sir." Unaccustomed to being the cynosure of strangers, she seemed relieved to find a familiar face emerging from the crowd.

While she fumbled in her reticule for her dance card, he greeted her mother and the colonel and they all moved into the ballroom. Taking the card, he saw that only the supper dance and a waltz remained unspoken for. All the other spaces were filled with the names of local gentlemen, in her own writing. He suspected that her modesty had prevented her filling in those two lines if no one had specifically requested them.

It was baconbrained of him, however irresistible, to tease Mimi by asking Harriet first. He had hoped for either a waltz or the supper dance with Mimi—but he was fairly sure now that she thought she had outfoxed him by filling her card.

"May I have both, Miss Cooper?" he requested. She blushed again, and nodded. She really was very pretty, in silver net over white satin, with Aunt Georgina's moonstones glimmering at her throat. Mimi had an eye for effect, he thought, turning to her. "Miss Lassiter, you will not be less kind than your friend?"

"Alas, sir, I cannot oblige." Triumphantly, she handed him her card.

Being forewarned, he perused it with more consideration than disappointment. His cousin was written down for the quadrille and a waltz, the same waltz that Simon had claimed from Harriet. Perhaps he wouldn't have to bribe the musicians. Gerald had appeared only once on Harriet's card. Given that he had been inveigled into the second dance with Mimi, no doubt he would be willing to exchange partners, if it could be done without the appearance of insult to Harriet.

He gave Mimi her card back. "It seems I'm too late," he admitted, trying to look mournful.

The best method of attack, he decided, was to consult Harriet first. That wasn't going to be easy, not because of the difficulty of separating the girls but because both were now engulfed in a swarm of partners and would-be partners. Fortunately the waltz was after supper, so he could speak to Harriet during their first dance.

Satisfied with his plan, he went off to inscribe his name on the cards of a number of unhappy damsels who already looked like wallflowers though the music had not yet started.

Dancing had been one of the things he enjoyed most in London, and he enjoyed it no less in the assembly room of the Derby Arms in Chester. The young ladies he stood up with were touchingly grateful. He did his best not to watch Mimi, though it was impossible not to be conscious of the whereabouts of that eye-catching scarlet gown. His was not the only gaze constantly drawn to her, he noticed. She seemed to be the focus of everyone's attention, as much for her gaiety as for her exotic beauty.

Once or twice he caught her glancing at him with a speculative look. It made him the more determined to win.

He found no opportunity to talk with Harriet before his dance with her came at last. Fortunately it was a country dance that allowed them periods of leisure for conversation while the other couples took their turns.

"Is this your first ball, Miss Cooper?" he asked.

"No, sir, I came to the Chester assembly last year, but it was not half so much fun without Mimi. She was at the Daumiers' ball in August, not long after she came to England, and that was much more enjoyable. Somehow she makes everything sparkle."

He glanced at the next set, where Mimi was curtsying to Mr. Blake. Judging by his bemused expression, the lawyer had got over his pique at being deprived of the quadrille.

"I was sorry to be too late to stand up with Miss Lassiter," he said, "though I was lucky enough to be just in time to sign your card."

"Forgive me, Mr. Hurst, but I believe . . . Oh!"

It was their turn to bow and curtsy, and then he had to wait for the rest of her words while first the ladies and then the gentlemen twirled in the center of the square.

"You were saying, ma'am?"

"I believe that in a sense Mimi owes you a dance?"

"She does indeed."

"I confess I do not understand why she is so unwilling to grant it, but it seems to me she is being a trifle unfair."

Simon knew perfectly well that it was Mimi's third obligation that hindered her performance of the second. She hadn't told even her best friend about the promised kiss, then, as he hadn't told Gerald and Aunt Georgina.

"Shockingly unfair," he said blandly as they finished the next figure.

"The Lassiters' evening gatherings were used to turn into informal hops quite often, but not since your arrival. It is not that she dislikes you, sir," Harriet added hastily.

"I'm glad to hear it. She has simply taken some maggot into her head. Perhaps she fears I'd tread on her toes?"

Harriet chuckled. "You are far less likely to do so than is Albert Pell. It is two hours since I danced with him, and I still feel the bruises."

They were separated again. He wondered whether she herself might suggest that he exchange dances with Gerald. She had probably seen Mimi's card. But no, she was too sensitive to risk hurting him by appearing to reject him, and too modest to risk appearing to claim a second dance with his lordship.

"Mimi is given to odd notions," she said at the next opportunity, "but I have never known her to be unkind."

"It's particularly unfair since my cousin has contrived to appropriate two dances with her."

That brought forth another chuckle. "Oh no, sir, he was forced into it."

"Then you think he wouldn't object to giving up the second? No, it's impossible, for then I'd lose my waltz with you."

"But once you have danced with Mimi, I daresay there will be dancing at the Lassiters' again, so we shall be able to stand up together there. If you truly wish it," she added, blushing.

"Of course I wish it," Simon said truthfully. The vicar's daughter was a sweet-natured girl, and he regretted manipulating her. She was by no means stupid, though, and he hoped she realized what he was about and appreciated his efforts to avoid insulting her. "Well, if you're willing, Gerald can have nothing to complain of since he'll gain the prettiest and most agreeable girl in the room as his partner." And that was true, too, for neither adjective fitted Mimi.

She was a bewitching and beautiful minx.

Simon had chosen the set he and Harriet were members of because it was close to where Lady Thompson sat chatting with her cronies. He knew Gerald, who had danced with no one but Harriet and Mimi, was taking their aunt in to supper. As the music ended, Gerald emerged from the card room and together the four went through to the supper room.

To Simon's relief, the room was crowded with small tables set for four. The last thing he wanted at present was to share a table with Mimi. She was at the far side of the room, near the buffet, with Albert Pell as her partner. The colonel and Mrs. Cooper were with them, so doubtless she would survive the experience.

When he and Gerald went to fill plates for their companions, Simon saw that Pell had already provided Mimi with a huge slice of egg-and-ham pie. She was looking at it in dismay.

"Whatever a *young* lady's appetite, she does not care to be seen overindulging in public," said Gerald, and proceeded to pile sweetmeats on Aunt Georgina's plate.

For Harriet, Simon chose a crabmeat vol-au-vent, salad, thin bread and butter, and a Bakewell tartlet. It looked too little for a young lady who had been dancing all evening. He was going to take some more bread and butter, then he bethought himself that the vicarage budget probably didn't run to crab or almonds, so he snabbled the last vol-au-vent and added another tart. He could always eat them himself if she didn't want them.

She was delighted with his selections. "Last year," she said, "I had supper with Mr. Pell and he brought me nothing but a slice of pie."

Laughing, he told her, "That's just what he's given Miss Lassiter now. Gerald, I want to waltz with Miss Lassiter."

"I wish you the best of luck, my dear fellow."

"You'll let me take your place?"

"On the contrary, I should not dream of insulting a lady by tamely surrendering a dance with her . . ."

"You didn't even ask her for the second dance," Simon pointed out.

"Let me finish. I was about to say . . . unless you have some irresistible inducement to offer?"

"That I have. Miss Cooper has graciously agreed to take her friend's place."

"Then there is no more to be said. Miss Cooper, allow me to congratulate you on your good taste in abjuring a dance with my cousin."

Harriet flushed. Lady Thompson leaned across the table and patted her hand.

"Don't let these odious wretches discompose you, my dear. They are just teasing each other."

With a warm smile for Harriet, Gerald said, "It was

indeed odious of Simon to put you in such a position. However, as I am to profit by his rudeness, I must beg you to forgive him."

"I do, my lord. How could I not forgive someone who provided me with such a delicious supper?"

The gentlemen both laughed, and her ladyship nodded approvingly.

"Let me fetch you a dish of syllabub, Miss Cooper," offered Simon, standing up, "just in case I need your forgiveness at some time in the future."

"I don't care for the sound of that," Gerald drawled. "Offend Miss Cooper again and you may find yourself facing a pistol at dawn."

"Nonetheless," Harriet said, "I should love a dish of syllabub."

"So should I," said Aunt Georgina.

Simon went back to the buffet. Glancing at Mimi's table, he saw that she had taken a few bites of pie and pushed it aside. Albert Pell was still eating, presumably a second or third helping, and the colonel and Mrs. Cooper were deep in conversation.

He was surprised that Mimi hadn't defied convention by helping herself at the buffet. Taking pity on her, he delivered a bowl of syllabub and was paid with a glowing look of gratitude.

Shortly after he returned to his table, the sound of a violin tuning up floated through from the ballroom. Sir Wilfred, resplendent in a turquoise-and-yellow-striped coat, came to remind Harriet that she was promised to him for the next set. It was one o'clock in the morning, and Lady Thompson was growing sleepy.

Simon and Gerald escorted her to a comfortable chair in an anteroom.

"Are you quite sure you had not rather leave now, Aunt?" Gerald asked.

"No, no, my dears. There are only two sets left, are there not? I daresay I shall nod a little, but I would not for the world deprive either of you of the last waltz. It has been a most interesting and instructive evening."

Her nephews looked at each other with raised eyebrows, but when they turned back to her ladyship to request elucidation she had her eyes firmly shut. They both shrugged their shoulders and went back to the ballroom to watch a minuet whose stately measures were well suited to the postprandial somnolence of which Lady Thompson was not the only victim.

In London the balls would be at their height, the gambling fever scarce begun, but provincial Chester was ready for bed.

Nor had provincial Chester quite made up its mind about the waltz, that daring new dance from the Continent. As Simon made his way toward Mimi after the minuet, he saw more than one tearful young lady pleading with a stern mama while a hopeful beau stood by awaiting permission to indulge in what amounted, in old-fashioned eyes, to a public embrace.

On the far side of the room, Gerald intercepted Harriet on her way back to her mother. Mimi, talking to the colonel and Mrs. Cooper, didn't notice her intended partner's defection.

Simon bowed to her and said, "My dance, I believe, Miss Lassiter."

"Oh no, Mr. Hurst." She looked taken aback. "I told you my card was completely full. I'm engaged to Lord Litton for the waltz."

"You were, to be sure. However, as you had earlier promised me a dance, Gerald and Miss Cooper generously agreed to give up their prior claims." Trying not to smile at the gathering storm signals in her face, he gestured to where the viscount and the vicar's daughter stood talking, waiting for the music to begin.

"How could they! I won't dance with you."

"Don't be a peagoose, Mimi," said her father. "Of course you will."

"But Papa . . ."

"That's enough nonsense." The colonel's voice was

quiet but his commanding tone would have made an erring subaltern jump to attention. His daughter was not proof against it.

"Yes, Papa."

Simon offered his arm. She laid her hand on it and silently they moved onto the floor. Victory somehow lost its sweetness.

"I'm sorry," he said. "It was not fair of me to force you to stand up with a bailiff's apprentice when you were promised to a viscount."

"That has nothing to do with it!" she flared up. "As though I care . . . But it was disgracefully underhanded in you, you must admit."

He smiled tentatively. "I freely admit it, Princess, and beg forgiveness."

"I shall take the matter under consideration," she said in the grand manner, then spoiled the effect by adding, "but I'll be da . . . bothered if I ever forgive Harriet or Lord Litton!"

The music started then. With her warm little hand in his and his arm about her supple waist, he swung her into the waltz in a swirl of scarlet and gold. There were few couples on the floor and he knew everyone was watching, probably wondering why the belle of the ball was in the arms of so shabby a fellow. He didn't care. It was worth every subterfuge.

"Thank you for bringing me the syllabub," she said, sounding oddly shy. "I was about to go and help myself."

"I was surprised you hadn't already done so."

"I didn't make loud comments about how insipid Sophia's dress looked, either. That was an even greater temptation, but I wouldn't lower myself to her level. And I didn't want all those strangers to blame Mrs. Cooper for my behavior when she was so kind as to relieve Mrs. Forbes of the onerous duty of chaperoning me."

"I daresay you're a sad trial to Mrs. Forbes, Princess. She's a trifle old-fashioned in her notions, I expect."

"She certainly is." Mimi was restored to her usual

cheerfulness. "Just think, she disapproves of the waltz."

"Then we can agree in disagreeing with her, can we not?"

"Oh, yes!"

Simon pulled her closer to him, perhaps an inch or two closer than strict propriety allowed, and whirled her about the room.

=14=

THE FULL MOON SHINING in through the carriage window revealed Lady Thompson slumbering cherubically in one corner. On the opposite seat her two nephews lounged, both wide awake despite the lateness of the hour.

"How Lady Elizabeth would sneer at such a country assembly," observed Gerald.

"Who?" asked Simon, abstracted.

"Lady Elizabeth Venables, only daughter of the Earl of Prestwitton, and Toast of the *Ton*." There was laughter in Gerald's voice. "You remember her?"

"Oh, yes. Sophia Marbury reminds me of her a bit."

"Sophia Marbury!" His lordship's yelp made his aunt stir and mutter a protest. He lowered his voice. "Good gad, how can you possibly equate the two?"

"Both are coldhearted, self-interested females, and I'm quite sure Miss Marbury would sneer at a country assembly if it weren't the best she can aspire to."

"I daresay she would."

"But you don't, coz? You the jaded exquisite, you the frequenter of the salons and ballrooms and clubs of the politest of the Polite World?"

"You wax unwonted eloquent, coz. No, I would not sneer. I confess to having suffered a certain tedium at times, but that is equally true of town entertainments. And there were compensations."

"I'd wager you mean my contest with Mimi," said Simon resignedly.

"That among other things, yes."

"I'm glad to have provided some amusement."

"She was quite the most striking young lady present, well worth your efforts. Did she resign herself to losing?"

"Oh yes, we parted friends." Simon fell silent, reliving the waltz. Mimi had accepted defeat gracefully, without resentment, as she had when he invited himself to dinner. She had seated him beside her then, and tonight she had moved feather-light in his arms, her dark eyes dreamy. What had she been dreaming of?

He had gained the dance and the dinner by subterfuge—paying her back in her own coin, he thought, smiling—but he wanted the kiss she still owed to be honestly won. And he wanted her to give it before she discovered that he was really the Earl of Derwent, heir to the Marquis of Stokesbury.

He wanted the princess to kiss the frog, and he was not at all sure that she ever would. For all her odd ways, Mimi was not one to bestow her favors freely.

"But I still owe him a kiss!" Mimi wailed.

"A kiss!" said Harriet, dropping her sewing in her shock. "You never promised him a kiss!"

"I wasn't thinking. I wanted my bracelet back, and I thought he was a stranger just passing through. I never thought he'd claim it."

"Perhaps he will not."

"He's already tricked me into inviting him to dinner and dancing with him. Oh, Harriet, I don't want to kiss anyone, but especially not Simon!"

"Why especially not Simon?"

Mimi blushed. "Because I'm trying to get him to offer for you, of course. You do want to marry him, do you not?"

"Yes, I suppose so." Harriet sighed. "I like him very well."

"You haven't gone and fallen in love with Lord Litton, have you?"

"He is like a dream come true, tall and handsome,

charming, courteous, so elegant and polished, and yet so kind. . . . I am half in love, Mimi, but I'm fighting against it, for I know there is no hope."

"Oh dear, I was afraid of this. I wish he had turned out to be as arrogant as I thought him. I wish he had never come here, at least not to stay."

"This is the first time I have had a chance to really come to know him. He usually stays at Mere House no longer than a few days."

"With any luck, he'll leave soon. Simon will stay, though, as he's learning from Mr. Wickham. He's not tall and handsome and elegant, but perhaps when you are not forever comparing him with the viscount you will find yourself able to love him."

Somehow this cheering thought failed to cheer either young lady. They sat in silent gloom. Somewhere in the house Judith was practicing a song. Through the open window, with the scent of lilac, floated the liquid warble of a blackbird and the chattering voices of Sally and Prue.

"They are helping Mama plant out the French bean seedlings," said Harriet. She picked up the pair of drawers she was hemming and set a few stitches while Mimi went to the window and looked out at the sunny garden.

The front door knocker sounded.

"Will one of the boys answer it?" asked Mimi.

"No, they went to the village green to test the cricket bat Ferdie sent Peter for his tenth birthday. Real Suffolk willow! And Judith is upstairs."

"Don't get up, I'll go." Mimi went out into the passage. The front door stood open to admit the early-summer warmth, and on the doorstep Sir Wilfred was just raising his hand to knock again.

"Servant, Miss Lassiter. Went up to the Hall and your butler told me you was at the vicarage."

"Waring was quite correct, as you see, sir. Did you wish to see me about anything in particular?"

"Proper thing to call on a young lady after dancing with her at a ball. Was going to call on Miss Cooper, too, of course."

"I see. I'd better go and find out if Harriet is at home." There was another ridiculous English convention, she thought. No wonder Sir Wilfred looked slightly surprised—she would not be here if Harriet was not. But Harriet would want to put away the drawers and take up some innocuous needlework before a gentleman was introduced into her presence.

Grateful for the warning, Harriet bundled the drawers into the mending basket, shoved the basket under a table, and took a piece of embroidery from her workbox. Mimi was about to go and invite Sir Wilfred to step in when Harriet shook her head.

"You are a guest, not a servant," she reminded her. "Sit down and look like a guest while I ask him in."

So Mimi disposed herself on the small sofa which was the smartest piece of furniture in the parlor, in what she hoped was a guestlike attitude. Really, a lack of servants did add unexpected complications to life!

She heard Lord Litton's voice in the passage and so was prepared when his lordship followed Harriet and Sir Wilfred into the little room. Harriet picked up her tambour hoop, sat down in the chair that sagged the worst, and invited the gentlemen to be seated. Sir Wilfred joined Mimi on the sofa, but Lord Litton, after a doubtful glance at the two remaining chairs, leaned against the mantelpiece.

"I see by your sparkling eyes and blooming cheeks, ladies, that you are both perfectly recovered from last night's dissipation," he observed.

"A country ball ain't much in the way of dissipation," Sir Wilfred pointed out. "Daresay you're dancing and gaming till dawn every night during the London Season, Litton."

"Oh, not quite every night. It becomes tedious, I assure you."

"I can imagine that it might," said Harriet, "but I confess I should like to dance more often. Last year Lord and Lady Daumier held an August ball at Highbury, when they came home from Brighton. Do you remember, Mimi?"

"It was my first ball ever. Every instruction Mrs. Forbes ever gave me about English Society vanished from my head. I'd never have survived it without your help, Harriet."

"The Daumiers ain't going to Brighton this year," Sir Wilfred announced. "Was talking to their bailiff the other day, expecting them home end of the month."

"I hope they have another ball," Mimi said. "Will you still be here at the end of the month, my lord? And Mr. Hurst?"

"I cannot speak for Simon, and my own plans are uncertain, I regret to say, Miss Lassiter. However, I know Daumier slightly, so if we are here no doubt we shall both attend. I left Simon with Wickham just now," the viscount continued. "He asked me to assure you, Miss Cooper, that he will be here shortly to pay his respects. No doubt that is he," he added as the door knocker sounded again.

Harriet and Mimi were both about to rise when they heard Judith's voice in the passage. A moment later, she ushered the Reverend Lloyd into the crowded room. She curtsied to the guests and was about to leave when Mimi stopped her.

"Don't go, Judith. It's time I was leaving, and you can sit with Harriet since your mama is busy outside."

Harriet protested, but Mimi was firm. Refusing Sir Wilfred's escort, she took her leave and was soon walking up the lane, feeling noble. For once Harriet should have all the gentlemen to herself, including Simon when he arrived.

The sun was warm between the sheltering hedges. Mimi took off her gloves and stuffed them in her reticule, took off her hat and swung it by the ribbons as she strolled along, pausing now and then to look at the flowers on the hedgebanks. Harriet had named them to her: the white stars of stitchwort, rosy ragged robin, a few late primroses, and tall stalks of cow parsley. Remembering her musical evening, Mimi giggled.

Reaching the gate, she climbed the stile beside it and

crossed the meadow, bright now with ox-eye daisies and golden buttercups, to the kissing gate in the next hedge. As she went through, she imagined a milkmaid meeting her swain there, leaning one each side of the free-swinging gate to exchange a kiss. What was it like to kiss a man? Not a good-night kiss such as she dropped on Papa's cheek every evening, but a true lover's . . .

Oh no! Simon was riding across the paddock toward her. Her face hot, she hurried to put some distance between herself and the kissing gate, crushing the delicate, palest-pink lady's smock blossoms beneath her feet as she sped to meet him.

He swung down from Intrepid's back. "Well met, Princess. I was on my way to the Hall to pay my duty call on the lady who did me the honor of standing up with me last night."

"Well, now that you have seen me your duty is done so you can go straight to the vicarage. Lord Litton is there and he said you were on your way."

"There's no rush. You're going home now? You ought not to walk alone, Princess."

"This is my father's land."

"But if you're coming from the vicarage, you have been walking in the public road."

Mimi couldn't tell him that she had felt safer in the public road than she did here alone with him. His closeness was oddly disturbing. If he chose to insist on taking his kiss, she wouldn't be able to stop him.

"Asota doesn't like walking, and Jacko had to take Deva Lal to the smithy to have a loose shoe nailed." Words were a barrier, she found. "Does it hurt a horse when the blacksmith bangs nails into its foot?"

"I've never known a horse object to being shod, unless by an incompetent smith, except for the first time a yearling is taken to the smithy. The noise and heat and fire must be frightening."

"I should like to see it, but Mrs. Forbes says a smithy is no place for a young lady."

"We're agreed that Mrs. Forbes is a trifle old-fashioned

in her notions of propriety, are we not? I can see no harm in it. Shall I take you one day?"

"Yes, please!"

"Very well. And now I'll escort you home."

"You cannot take Intrepid up the ha-ha wall," she pointed out, "and the other way is too far to walk. You had best go on to the vicarage."

"I'll leave Intrepid grazing here. Come, Princess, let us take a look at our livestock and crops."

As they talked they had moved toward the pond. Now Simon turned Intrepid loose, then joined Mimi on the bank.

The flags were still flowering, the rushes thriving, and some of the watercress had at last decided to take root and produce a few insignificant white flowers. There was a patch of pale-blue forget-me-nots, too, and marsh marigolds, which must have been growing in the boggy ground before the pond was dug.

"It's looking very pretty," Mimi said with satisfaction, "and the tadpoles must be happy, because they get bigger every day. But their gills have shrunk. Is that why they keep coming to the surface with their mouths open?"

"I expect so. If their gills are gone, they will need to breathe air." Simon took off his gloves and stuffed them in his pocket. Crouching at her side, he put his hand in the water and managed to scoop up a tadpole. They examined it as it wriggled in his palm. "You see those knobs where the gills were, just behind the head? Those will grow into legs soon."

He dropped it back into the pond and it dashed away. Mimi stood up.

"I must go and see if mine at home are beginning to grow legs. I didn't really look when I fed them yesterday."

"It's about time we changed their water," said Simon. "I'll come and help."

She smiled at him, comfortable with him again. She'd done her best to send him to the vicarage, and she couldn't help it if he was more interested in tadpoles than in Harriet. Not that she meant to give up.

At the top of the stone steps they took the gravel path past the gazebo, across wide lawns and through the gardens to the ornately patterned house.

"I thought Harriet looked particularly lovely last night," Mimi observed as they walked. Just in time she stopped herself from saying that it was a pity her friend had so few pretty gowns. Simon was not likely to be able to provide for his wife the luxuries the vicar could not afford for his daughter. "She is such a graceful dancer, and white becomes her."

"She looked very pretty. How fortunate that her cool moonlight complemented your blazing sunshine so splendidly."

"We did cause quite a stir when we entered the ballroom, did we not? Poor Sophia with her seed pearls that she was so proud of! But you must not think, because Harriet appears cool and her manners are reserved, that she is not a truly warm and loving person."

"I don't think it, Princess. Any more than I think, because you enjoy setting local society by the ears, that you don't know how to behave with propriety."

"I had better put on my hat before Mrs. Forbes sees me," said Mimi guiltily.

"It seems a pity not to, when it's such a fetching confection." Simon took the wide-brimmed straw Leghorn hat with its bunch of cherries, set it on her head, and tied the broad cherry-colored ribbons under her chin.

The back of his hand brushed her cheek and his head bent toward her, lips slightly parted. Mimi's heart went pit-a-pat, her breath caught in her throat—and then he stepped back.

Carefully not meeting his gaze as she adjusted the ribbons for comfort, she scolded herself: for her agitation, for not trusting him, most of all for feeling a trifle regretful that he hadn't kissed her. Only the merest trifle, of course. She was really excessively glad that she had misinterpreted his intentions.

They walked on. Under cover of her hat-brim, she glanced at him sideways. No, he was not as handsome as Gerald Litton, but he had a pleasing face, open and friendly. She couldn't understand why Harriet preferred the starchy viscount.

"It's too warm for gloves," she said.

"Yes, I shan't put mine on," he agreed.

They went directly to the scullery through the kitchen court. Changing the tadpoles' water was by now a polished operation that took them only a few minutes. The casseroled tadpoles, like their free brethren, were losing their gills and thinking seriously about growing legs.

"It's still hard to believe they are going to turn into frogs," Mimi said as she crumbled some stale bread into the water and watched them flock to gobble it down.

"It's a law of nature," Simon assured her. "Tadpoles turn into frogs, and frogs turn into princes."

"Gracious, what *shall* I do with a scullery full of princes?" Laughing, she led the way into the kitchen.

"Tha'll be wanting a drop o' lemonade after walking in t' heat, Miss Mimi," suggested Cook. "And a glass of ale for t' gentleman? Mr. Waring s'll bring it to t' drawing room along o' madam's tea."

"Thank you, Cook, that sounds good," said Mimi, but as the kitchen door shut behind them she added severely, "And as soon as you have drunk your ale, Mr. Hurst, you must be on your way to the vicarage. You are expected."

He saluted, laughing at her. "Aye, aye, Cap'n."

They joined Mrs. Forbes in the drawing room, where she was knitting gray worsted stockings for the Poor Basket. As usual she was silent in company, but Mimi and Simon chatted about the assembly until Waring brought in the refreshments.

As soon as Simon finished his ale and a slice of Cook's sticky, spicy Yorkshire parkin, Mimi reminded him, "You are expected at the vicarage, Mr. Hurst, and Intrepid will be wondering what has become of you."

"I'm on my way, Miss Lassiter," he said obediently, and bowed to Mrs. Forbes. "Your servant, ma'am."

She nodded coolly. As soon as the drawing-room door closed behind him, she turned to Mimi and said, "I am glad to see you discouraging Mr. Hurst's attentions. He will not do for you at all."

"He is only a friend, ma'am, not a suitor. Indeed, he makes no attempt to flirt with me, nor to fix his interest. But surely he is no less eligible than Mr. Blake and Mr. Lloyd, a lawyer and a parson?"

"Most certainly he is. A lawyer is an independent man, and one must always respect a man of the cloth, whereas a bailiff can never be more than a superior servant. Not that I consider either of those gentlemen good enough to be your husband, though your papa refuses to discourage them."

"Papa just wants me to choose for myself."

"You will not refuse the guidance of an older and wiser head, however. All three are no better than fortune hunters. My dear, with your fortune and your royal background—unfortunately foreign, but royal nonetheless!—you may certainly aim at a title."

"But I don't want to marry Sir Wilfred."

"Sir Wilfred is a mere country baronet, for all his foppery. What say you to Viscount Litton?"

"Lord Litton! I cannot believe he is the least bit interested in me."

"Come now, Mimi, the colonel told me you were one of only two young ladies his lordship danced with last night, and you cannot suppose he has any interest in a parson's daughter." Mrs. Forbes grew quite pink-cheeked with excitement. "Besides, has he not stayed at Mere House for several weeks now, when his usual visit is no more than a few days? What else should keep him here?"

"He has shown no sign of partiality," Mimi insisted.

"La, my dear, he is too well-bred a gentleman to raise hopes where he is not perfectly decided. I consider that you have a very good chance of receiving an offer, if you will only look kindly upon him. Needless to say, I would not have you set your cap at him in a vulgar way, but oh, Mimi, do try to behave with propriety in his presence. I declare, I cannot think what has come over you recently, and nothing is so likely to give a gentleman with such polished manners a disgust of you as the least hint of indecorum."

"I'm sure you are right, ma'am, but I don't really want to marry his lordship either."

Leaving her chaperon tut-tutting, Mimi wandered to the window and looked out over the gardens to the gazebo and the spread of green meadows beyond. What was the difference, she wondered, between a nobleman to whom her fortune made her an acceptable bride, and a bailiff who would wed her for her fortune?

The viscount had more choice, she supposed. He must have countless wealthy beauties flung at his head in town, so he might be expected to have better reasons for his selection than just wealth. Whereas to Simon hers might be the only fortune within reach.

Not that he gave any indication of wanting either her or her fortune—or why had he not kissed her in the garden?

=15=

PRIM AND PROPER IN her faded sprig muslin and straw bonnet, Harriet sat on the bench under the chestnut tree on the village green and wished she were three years younger.

The children were having such fun with Peter's new cricket bat. After a few minutes as a spectator, Judith had forgotten her aspirations to young-ladyhood and joined in—but she was only fifteen. Three village children, watching with envious eyes, had been invited by Peter to take part, so they were four a side.

"That's enough for a halfway decent game," Peter told Harriet importantly, "if Prue wasn't so little."

Prue had the bat at present, fortunately one of the new, shorter bats which didn't quite dwarf her. She stood proudly in front of a wicket composed of one old stump of Ferdie's, a forked stick, and a twig balanced across the top. Nor did the ball match the splendor of the new bat, being an aged sphere of India-rubber with a hole in one side where some dog had chewed on it. It hardly seemed to matter.

Jimmy was bowling to his little sister. Harriet was glad to see he took her age into consideration as he ran up and rolled the ball along the ground toward her. Prue struggled to lift the bat, the village boy playing wicket-keeper crouching behind her with a grin, sure of getting her out. To everyone's astonishment, bat and ball connected. Prue herself was far too surprised to run, and

Sally, with the ball bouncing toward her, forgot she was supposed to catch it.

"Oh, well done, Prue!" she shouted, jumping up and down.

Harriet laughed and cheered and waved her parasol.

"An admirable hit," observed a voice close beside her.

"My lord! I did not see you coming."

"I beg your pardon if I startled you, Miss Cooper." The viscount stood with one hand, gloved in the best York tan, on the back of the bench, the other holding his horse's reins. "I did not want to spoil the batsman's concentration."

She smiled at him, relieved that she had not given in to the temptation to pin up her skirts and join the game.

At that moment Peter ran up. With the sketchiest of bows to Lord Litton, he burst into speech. "Harriet, Jim says Prue can't count a run, but she's only little, she just forgot, it's not fair. Tell him not to be mean."

"Oh dear, it does seem unfair, but there are rules."

"It's not a proper game, after all. We've only got one wicket 'cause we've only got one bat. The other's just a mark on the ground."

"Let me suggest a solution," proposed the viscount. "Instead of dividing into teams, you could all be fielders except the batsman, who only has to hit the ball to score a run. If he or she also runs to the mark, that counts for two runs. And you all take turns, in alphabetical order perhaps, at bat."

"That sounds all right, sir," said Peter doubtfully, "except that everyone will have to remember their own score and some will forget and some might cheat."

"I shall keep score," Lord Litton promised. As Peter returned to the wicket, he looped his horse's reins over a branch, took a small leather-bound diary and pencil from his pocket, and sat down beside Harriet. "I trust you can tell me the names of the village boys, ma'am?" he queried.

"Yes, of course." She told him, and he wrote them down. "But you cannot wish to stay here, sir."

"Can I not? I beg to differ, Miss Cooper. What could be pleasanter on a warm summer's day than to lounge in the shade with a pretty young lady, watching a sporting event?"

Harriet blushed. "A sporting event of no significance, my lord."

"Then let us give it some significance with a wager. I will lay you odds on Miss Sally scoring highest, for I know her to be a spirited young lady."

"Oh no, Jimmy is sure to win, for he was used to play with Ferdie."

"There we are, then: if young James wins, I shall buy you a fan; if Miss Sally, you shall sing to me when next we meet at Salters Hall."

Harriet was afraid that Papa would strongly disapprove of her entering into a wager with a gentleman, but the stakes seemed innocent—and flattering. "A plain, ordinary fan," she said, looking up at him. "Not too expensive."

"A plain, ordinary fan it shall be," he promised gravely, then grinned. "You are very confident of winning."

"I am. Recall that Sally had to be rescued from that tree, for all her spirit! Look, poor Prue is out. I expect she will come over here."

"No, that is the beauty of the game I proposed. Since all are fielders, no one has to sit about doing nothing while awaiting a turn. We used to play that way at Crossfields, because my eldest sister was wont to escape from the field of combat if left to her own devices."

"Your sisters played cricket with you?"

"And my brothers. I have almost as many of each as you do."

Before Harriet could decide whether it would be impertinent to ask for more details of his lordship's family, Mimi and Mr. Hurst rode up, followed by Jacko. Mr. Hurst dismounted and helped Mimi down from Deva Lal's back.

"Good morning, Harriet, my lord," she cried. "We are on our way to the smithy, but I wanted to watch the game first. I must say it doesn't look quite the same as when Papa's sepoys played cricket."

"What are sepoys?" Harriet asked.

"Indian soldiers in the British army."

"Oh yes, I think you have told me before. I expect they had two bats and two proper wickets and a proper ball."

"And white uniforms and an umpire," added the viscount. "But this is the way we used to play at Crossfields, eh, Simon?"

"Yes, and I've half a mind to join in."

A ball hit by one of the village boys sailed their way at that moment. Jacko put out a hand, caught it, and sent it whizzing back to Jimmy. The groom looked pleadingly at Mimi.

"Go on, Jacko, go and play," she urged.

"I'm going too," Simon decided, shrugging out of his coat and dropping it on the grass. "Coming, Gerald?"

To Harriet's surprise, Lord Litton cast her a rueful glance and took off his superb brown riding jacket, not without difficulty. "I cannot resist, Miss Cooper," he said, folding the coat carefully and draping it over the back of the bench. "Guard this with your life, keep score, and pray do not tell any of my London acquaintances what you are seeing!" He strode toward the players, a splendid figure in his white shirt, buff waistcoat, and tan buckskins.

"Help me pin up my skirt, Harriet," Mimi requested. "If Judith can play, so can I."

"But Judith is still in the schoolroom," Harriet protested, to no avail. Mimi departed, leaving her sitting wistfully alone again, decorous but far from content.

It was Sally's turn to bat. Gerald Litton bowled to her, running up with his usual easy grace and sending her straight, gentle balls off which she managed to score two runs before being caught out. She and Prue came to join Harriet. Tired, they wanted to sit quietly and make daisy chains.

So Sally had not won. That meant Lord Litton owed Harriet a fan. Once again she was racked with doubt about the propriety of their wager.

With the little girls' departure, the game had speeded up. Simon took the bat, and Gerald's languid bowling became demonic. The ball flew so hard and fast, Harriet had trouble following its course. Simon scored two fours, even the fielders applauding, then two singles as Gerald became wilier. Then Mimi fielded a hit and managed to throw it straight enough for Jimmy, at wicket-keeper, to knock Simon out.

"I cannot believe my eyes!" said a voice at Harriet's ear.

She jumped. "Oh, Mr. Lloyd, you startled me. I beg your pardon, what did you say?"

The vicar of Highbury was staring at the players with an expression of horrified distaste on his round face. "I cannot believe my eyes," he repeated. "How undignified, how utterly unsuited to the wife of a clergyman. Miss Lassiter's behavior has been odd of late, but to see her running about in public with her limbs revealed to all and sundry is the outside of enough. My dear Miss Cooper, I cannot sufficiently commend your maidenly modesty, your virtuous dignity."

As he spoke, Harriet had taken a paper of pins from her reticule. Now, with increasing indignation, she began to pin her skirts up above her ankles. "I have been longing to play," she told him, "but someone had to guard his lordship's coat and keep score. Pray be seated, Mr. Lloyd. Here is the score book, and be so good as to keep an eye on Sally and Prue, if you please."

Half defiant, half aghast at her own boldness, she left him spluttering. Unsure where to go, she moved tentatively onto the field of play. Gerald Litton was nearby, his back to her. Then Mimi waved to her and he turned.

"Miss Cooper!" He grinned at her. "I am delighted to see that you, too, found it impossible to resist the temptation."

"I did not mean to play, but Mr. Lloyd said such odious things about Mimi . . ."

"You are a loyal friend. Lloyd would do well to study your father's tolerance and compassion." His smile was understanding.

"Well, I do think it un-Christian of him to be so condemnatory. I told him to guard your coat."

Gerald chuckled. "Ah, that is both an admirable setdown for him and a weight off my mind. I feared you had left it to fend for itself."

Harriet thoroughly enjoyed the game, though she spent more time chatting to Mimi than actually doing anything productive. She took her turn at bat, and with memories of Ferdie's coaching in her youth managed to score a couple of runs. The overall winner of the day, however, was Jacko. Even with Gerald and Simon conspiring against him, he hit three sixes, a four, and several singles. To his delight, the viscount gave him a guinea prize.

"So neither of us has won," Harriet said to Gerald as they returned to the bench at the end of the game.

"On the contrary, ma'am, both of us have lost. Therefore, I owe you a fan and you owe me a song. Agreed?"

Shyly she agreed.

Mr. Lloyd rose as they approached. "I fear, Miss Cooper, I was unable to fathom your method of scoring," he said with punctilious politeness. "Your little sisters, as you see, have not wandered. Here is your coat, my lord," he added somewhat acidly, holding it up.

"I thank you, sir," said his lordship and turned his back, thus virtually forcing the parson to help him into his coat.

Harriet could not quite approve of such cavalier treatment, despite the vicar's obnoxious behavior. She was about to say something to soothe his ruffled feelings when Gerald addressed her.

"Miss Cooper, I am dreadfully afraid there may be a wrinkle or two on my back. If I were to sit down on the bench, would you be so kind as to smooth out any you espy?"

The superfine cloth stretched creaseless across his broad shoulders. Nonetheless, Harriet had met another temptation she couldn't resist. Running her hands over the muscular back beneath the elegant coat, she was lost. And doubly lost when he reached back, took one of her hands, and carried it forward to kiss it.

It was too late to pretend she was half in love with the viscount. He had her heart, her whole heart.

"I shall be miserable for the rest of my life," Harriet wailed. "I shall have to choose between living a spinster or marrying someone other than the man I love."

"Fustian," said Mimi briskly. "If you've fallen in love with him despite all your efforts, I shall just have to change my aim. It's not as if he were an earl or a marquis or a duke. Why should not a viscount marry where he will?"

"I have nothing to offer him."

"You have yourself, and you are the sweetest-natured girl, and pretty, and always neatly dressed and properly behaved."

"Except for playing cricket yesterday."

"That didn't give him a disgust of you. It seemed to me he was well pleased when you joined in, and I saw him kiss your hand when you helped with his coat."

Harriet blushed. "He hates to be untidy."

"So do you," Mimi pointed out. "It's my belief he likes you very well. He has no need of a fortune, and you are of gentle birth, so his family can have no real objection."

"Do you really think not?"

"Simon says they are charming people. On the way to the blacksmith's, we were talking about the cricket games they used to play at Crossfields and he told me all about Gerald's mama and brothers and sisters. His father died when he had barely reached his majority, so he had to help his mama bring them up. He has a brother in the army, and one still at school, and a sister at school, and two married sisters with children. Oh, that gives me a famous idea!"

"What is it, Mimi? What are you planning now?" Harriet asked nervously.

"You must spend more time with him, to give him a chance to fall in love with you. He likes children, does he not? He shall take you to visit Maria."

"I cannot possibly ask him to take me to Maria's!"

"No, but I shall work it out, just wait and see," said Mimi, full of confidence in her powers of persuasion.

"How very fortunate for me," Lord Litton remarked, "that Colonel Lassiter's carriage wheel needs repair on just the day Miss Lassiter had promised to take you to see your sister."

Harriet didn't know where to look. She was quite sure he had seen through Mimi's ruse, and could only pray that he didn't suppose she had anything to do with it. To her relief, his lordship's attention was on his horses as he drove his curricle through the narrow winding lanes.

"And fortunate for me, sir," she responded, plucking up courage, "that you brought your curricle to Cheshire even though you prefer to ride when you are in the country. Nothing can be pleasanter than driving in an open carriage on a sunny June day."

"Especially after just enough rain to damp down the dust without making the roads muddy." He smiled down at her. "When the wild roses are blooming, I wonder why anyone would choose to spend June in town."

They chatted for a while about flowers, then Harriet gathered her courage to say, "My lord, I know you told Papa you do not wish to hear any expression of thanks, but I cannot keep silent. Your generous offer to build an addition onto the vicarage . . ."

"Hush!" he commanded. "It is the plain duty of those with livings in their gift to ensure the comfort of the incumbents. I only wish I had realized sooner how inadequate the vicarage is for your family. I fear, however," he added, with a laugh in his voice, "that I have presented Mrs. Cooper with something of a quandary."

"Yes, she simply cannot decide which part of her garden she can spare to be built on."

"I confess that I have been teasing her a little. There is no reason why some part of the meadow behind the house should not be enclosed and added to the garden."

"Sir, you are too kind!" Harriet cried, overwhelmed.

"We frivolous fellows must do something to justify our

existence. Tell me, what are your thoughts on the colonel's orphanage? My aunt is throwing herself heart and soul into the project, and I understand Mr. Cooper is also involved."

The rest of the way to Maria's, about an hour's journey, they talked of the planned orphanage. Lord Litton was flatteringly interested in Harriet's opinions and ideas.

"Thank you, Miss Cooper," he said as the curricle drew up in front of the Talmadges' manor house. "I had never considered the subject before, but now I shall be able to discuss it with some show of intelligence. It is so very lowering to appear totally ignorant."

His groom jumped down and ran to take the horses' heads. The viscount helped Harriet down as Maria emerged from the house, calling a greeting, her two toddlers shyly at her heels.

Harriet was apprehensive that his lordship would be bored by a day spent in her sister's household. However, he soon won over the children and seemed to enjoy playing with them. When George Talmadge, a bluff country squire, joined them for luncheon, the gentlemen talked of crops and herds, and afterward went out together to inspect the Talmadge acres.

Naturally, Maria was full of curiosity about Harriet's noble companion. Harriet hoped she managed to persuade her that his bringing her was purely a gallant gesture, and practically forced on him by Mimi. When she described how Mimi had extorted two dances at the assembly from Lord Litton, Maria laughed and agreed that nothing could be read into the viscount's escort.

They returned to Salters Green in the late afternoon. Lord Litton drew up his team before the vicarage gate and reached into his coat pocket.

"You must think me very remiss at paying my debts," he said, "when you sang to me so delightfully the other evening. Here you are. I trust it is sufficiently plain for you."

Harriet fumbled a little as she unwrapped the tissue paper and took out a fan. The sticks were varnished bamboo, quite plain enough to satisfy scruples—and to disap-

point. Opening it, she found an exquisitely delicate painting of wild roses, palest pink on white parchment. There
was nothing half so lovely in the shops of Salters Green;
he must have gone to Nantwich or Chester to buy it.

"Oh," she breathed, "it is quite, quite perfect."

"When the wild roses are blooming," he quoted himself—was he looking at her flushed cheeks?— "I wonder
why anyone would choose to spend June in town."

Taking his hand to descend from the curricle, Harriet
knew that, if she never saw him again, as long as she
lived she would remember this day.

After a day spent with Wickham, Simon left Intrepid
in the Mere House stables and went into the house. He
reached the entrance hall just as Gerald came through
the front door.

"Have you had a pleasant day, coz?" he asked, grinning. "I've never seen anyone so neatly maneuvered.
Mimi's something of an expert, of course."

"Miss Lassiter is a kindhearted girl," said Gerald enig-
matically.

Before Simon could inquire as to his meaning, Baird
appeared and scooped a couple of letters off the hall
table.

"The post, my lord," he announced. "If you want your
letters presented on a silver salver, I fear you will be
forced to wait a few minutes, as I'm cleaning it."

"Ah, yes, I seem to recall that one of the vital duties of
a butler is cleaning the silver," said Gerald. "Hand them
over, man."

"My lord." Bowing, Baird complied.

Gerald glanced at the addresses as he and Simon headed
up the stairs to change. "Oh lord," he groaned, "one from
my mother. And one from Billings, who, I surmise, has
been forced to divulge my whereabouts. I daresay my sins
were bound to find me out sooner or later."

"Sins?" Simon asked, still puzzling over his cousin's
description of Mimi.

"You may recall, coz, that I left the makings of a scandal behind me in town and retreated here to avoid Mama's interrogation. The tabbies will have informed her long since that I encouraged Lady Elizabeth to hope for an offer and then abandoned her." Waving to Simon to follow, he went into his dressing room, took a paper knife from his dressing table, and broke open both seals.

"Oh yes, Lady Elizabeth. But that was ages ago—it seems like another lifetime."

"A nine-days wonder, no doubt; she will have snared another suitor by now. But Mama will want the full story from my lips. Yes, a pressing request that I satisfy her curiosity in person." He turned to the second letter. "Now what has Billings to say in excuse for disobeying my instructions?"

"I suppose you had to tell your agent where you were going in case of an emergency."

"Precisely, my dear fellow. There are matters it is unfair to expect an employee to take responsibility for, such as a row of cottages burned to the ground and three families homeless. Mama was in despair and Billings had to tell her he knew where to find me."

"That seems reasonable. You can't expect Aunt Cecilia to deal with such a disaster alone."

"No, I shall have to go to Crossfields, alas. I shall leave at dawn tomorrow. Do you go with me?"

"I can't leave now." If he went away, Simon felt, he would somehow forfeit the kiss Mimi owed him. "No, I still have much to learn from Wickham."

"You will also learn from watching me deal with this matter, you know, and I shall be coming back as soon as possible."

"Coming back to Cheshire?" Simon asked in surprise. "Why? You usually only come for a few days, and you've been here for weeks."

"I want to make sure Aunt Georgina does not sell everything she owns to endow Colonel Lassiter's orphanage." Though he laughed, Gerald sounded distinctly evasive to Simon's ears. "So, given that I shall return, will you come to Crossfields?"

"It would be far too complicated to keep switching between my aliases." Now Simon sounded evasive to his own ears. "I'd be bound to get caught out. No, I'll stay. Give my love to Aunt Cecilia." He departed for his own chamber.

Simon rose early next morning to see his cousin off. Watching him canter down the drive, he found his thoughts once more reverting to the puzzle that had kept him awake last night.

Gerald had once called Mimi a tiresome child; now he considered her a kindhearted girl. Gerald usually spent June in London and Brighton; now he proposed to return to Cheshire as soon as possible. Could the two be connected?

Surely Gerald wasn't planning to offer for Simon's princess!

=16=

THE SULTRY HEAT AND the towering clouds gathering over the gazebo promised a storm by evening, but Mimi and Harriet didn't care. Mimi gazed gloomily at the dead brown flowers on the lilac bushes, symbols of the hopes that had bloomed so recently and withered so soon.

"I really thought he would come to love you so much he didn't care about being a lord," she said. "I'm sorry he's gone, Harriet."

"It was too much to expect." Harriet tried to smile. "If all your plans succeeded, you would grow odiously conceited. But I have you to thank for a wonderful day with him, one I shall never forget."

"That's all very well, but I shan't let you wither away into a blighted old maid. Once you are married, with children of your own to care for, Gerald Litton will become a romantic memory, to treasure, not to pine over. I've let my campaign lapse but it can easily be started up again."

"Sir Wilfred and the others have started calling at the vicarage again. Even Mr. Lloyd has forgiven me for playing cricket."

"Yes, but he's forgiven me, too. Nothing I've done has put any of them off for long. I must think of something that will . . ." Mimi faltered, but went on resolutely, ". . . that will make Simon avoid me, as well as the rest. I know he could make you happy. Only he doesn't seem

148

to take offense whatever I do, so it will have to be something truly shocking."

"Oh no, Mimi, pray do not."

"Shh, let me think." She shivered as a moisture-laden breeze whisked through the gazebo, then the air was still and hot again. The expectant tension in the air reminded her of waiting for the monsoon to break in Bharadupatam. The temples would be full of offerings of flowers and sweetmeats, and dancers hired by farmers to please the gods and persuade them to release the life-bringing rains.

"Mimi . . ."

"Just a moment." She held up her hand. "I have it! We shall have dancing at Salters Hall one evening next week."

Harriet looked at once disappointed and relieved. "That will be delightful," she said, sounding doubtful, "even if Lord Litton is not here. But what shall you do? Step on your partners' toes?"

"Much better than that." Mimi giggled, restored to cheerfulness by the brilliance of her plan. "I shall perform an Indian dance."

"What sort of dance?" Suspicious, Harriet probed for more information, but Mimi refused to explain.

"You will see," she said mysteriously. "Can you come on Tuesday evening? Good, then I'll go and start writing invitations right away."

"Now, lad," Mrs. Wickham greeted Simon, "I don't want you thinking I approve of assignations, but I know you for an honorable gentleman as won't bring trouble to a young lady. Better you should meet in my parlor—just the once, mind, being as she said it were urgent—than off in the fields somewheres."

"Miss Lassiter wants to see me? Why on earth would she come here?"

"Nay, 'tis Miss Cooper. Never say you're after courting the both of them!"

"Certainly not, Mrs. Wickham, you need not look so

shocked. I can't imagine what Miss Cooper wants."

"Well, she's waiting in the parlor, lad, so go and find out. Leave the door open, mind."

Grinning affectionately at his mentor's plump wife, Simon obeyed.

Harriet was standing by the window of the comfortable chintz parlor, gazing out at the neat rows of vegetables in the back garden. She turned as he entered and came toward him, looking anxious and uncertain.

"Mr. Hurst, I beg your pardon for arranging this . . . this unconventional meeting. I am at my wits' end."

Taking her hand, he led her to a chair. "Sit down, Miss Cooper, and tell me what I may do for you. I'm entirely at your service." He took a seat opposite her.

"You will think me impertinent. Indeed, I ought to have approached Colonel Lassiter, and you may tell me I must do so, but . . . but . . ."

"I'm flattered that you find me more approachable than the colonel. This matter has something to do with Mimi, I take it?"

"I am so worried about her. I fear the colonel will either take offense, or laugh off my concern, and Mrs. Forbes has little influence over her, you know. You have received an invitation to the Hall for this evening?"

"Yes, an informal dance, I gather. What is she up to?" Simon hid a smile, finding it difficult to take Harriet's apprehensions seriously. He liked the vicar's daughter, but her notions of propriety were decidedly straitlaced by his reckoning.

"She means to do something scandalous."

He saw a chance to find out what Mimi hoped to gain by her singular behavior. "Tell me, Miss Cooper—I'm sure she confides in you—what's her purpose in doing her best to set up the backs of the entire neighborhood?"

Harriet flushed scarlet. "She is doing it for my sake," she said in a low voice, looking down at her hands, tightly clasped in her lap.

"Pray don't tell me if it embarrasses you," Simon hastened to assure her, more curious than ever.

"No, since I have asked your help, I owe you an explanation. You see, before the Lassiters came to Salters Green, several young gentlemen in the neighborhood were ... were courting me. But when Mimi arrived, they all switched their allegiance to her. So she decided to try to give them all a disgust of her so that they would come back to me."

Simon's heart sang. What a darling Mimi was, what a generous, kindhearted friend! Then he remembered that Gerald, too, had at last recognized her merits. His euphoria faded. As earl, and heir to a marquisate, he had been preferred over his cousin by the Incomparable Lady Elizabeth. As a humble bailiff, how could he hope that Mimi would choose him rather than the viscount?

And Harriet clearly expected him to put a stop to whatever scheme Mimi presently had in mind. That would scarcely endear him to her.

Though these thoughts flashed through his mind, his silence had been noticeable. Poor Harriet looked ready to sink. Simon leaned across and squeezed her hand gently.

"Thank you for explaining, Miss Cooper. You may trust me to keep it in strictest confidence. Now will you tell me what exactly your enterprising friend has in mind for the delectation of her guests this evening?"

He wouldn't have thought it possible for her cheeks to grow any redder, but they did.

"She would not tell me precisely, but I have gathered several hints. I believe she means to perform a ... an indecent dance!" she burst out, and hid her flaming face in her hands.

"Good gad!" Simon had traveled the world. He had seen belly dancers in Egypt and the equally erotic street and temple dancers of India. The idea of Mimi appearing in an English drawing room in their traditional garb, let alone performing, appalled him as thoroughly as the innocent Harriet could have wished. "Good gad," he repeated, rising to take an agitated turn about the room, "thank heaven you had the sense and the courage to come to me."

"Do you think you can stop her?"

"I can but hope so. If she's ignored your protests, I don't believe it will be the least use expostulating with her beforehand. We'll have to keep a close watch on her this evening and trust that between us we can nip her activities in the bud."

"You will not inform the colonel?"

"No, I think not. I know he's able to curb her with a word, but he's an indulgent father and after so long in India I'm not sure he understands what's acceptable in England. No, it's up to the two of us. I'll rely on you to watch her as carefully as I shall myself, and warn me if you see anything untoward."

"Oh, yes, I will. Thank you, sir." Harriet stood up and he came to take her hands. She looked up at him shyly. "You cannot imagine what a load you have taken from my mind."

He grinned down at her. "Being Miss Lassiter's friend is a heavy burden at times, is it not? One might say that she is not an example of still waters running deep, but rather of a roaring torrent running deep."

"One never knows quite what to expect next," she agreed, "but I would not have you think I would change her in any particular."

"Nor I, Miss Cooper, nor I," he assured her.

Simon recognized the spark of mischief in Mimi's eyes as he followed Aunt Georgina into the Lassiters' drawing room. She looked no different from the evening when she had played the sitar to much the same group of people, except that she was wearing an evening gown instead of a sari. Of a deep sea-green, it broke in a froth of white lace about her ankles. Pearls glowed against her dark skin at throat, wrists, and ears, and in her black hair.

"A goddess of the southern seas," he complimented her as he bowed over her hand.

He was overheard by Mr. Lloyd, entering behind him, who muttered something about not expecting blasphemy from an Englishman born and bred.

She wrinkled her enchanting little nose at Simon, and he winked at her before she turned to the parson. Harriet must be mistaken, he decided. Mimi couldn't possibly be so calm if she were about to commit an unforgivable vulgarity before the greater part of her acquaintance.

He greeted the colonel and went on into the room. The blue and gray carpet had been rolled to one end, exposing the polished oak floor for dancing, and the furniture was arranged around the walls.

Simon saw that Harriet had already arrived. Making his way to her, he whispered, "I cannot believe she is planning anything outrageous. She's perfectly at ease."

"She does not understand," Harriet said, looking up at him pleadingly.

She would have said more, but her father came up at that moment and spoke to Simon. Some minutes passed before he was able to turn back to Harriet and reassure her with a smile, "Don't worry, our compact holds."

The room was filling as the rest of the guests arrived. With a card table set up at one end, there was space for no more than four couples to stand up, Simon saw. Including himself, the usual five young gentlemen were present. Judith Cooper had come, and the Marburys had brought a chubby young lady, a cousin staying with them, so there were five young ladies also.

Mimi was aware of the problem. She joined Simon and Harriet at that moment and said, "I needn't request your cooperation, Mr. Hurst, as one can always find a gentleman willing to sit out a dance, but Harriet, I hope you and Judith won't mind taking a turn as wallflowers. I cannot ask Sophia or her cousin. I daresay it's the duty of a hostess to yield the floor to her guests, but I should like to stand up once or twice."

"Of course," Harriet said. "I shall go and speak to Judith at once."

She and Simon exchanged speaking glances. As long as Mimi was dancing with a partner, presumably she couldn't get up to anything too dreadful. The moments they must watch out for were the sets she sat out.

Mrs. Cooper had opened the harpsichord and was looking through the music.

"May I have the first dance, Princess?" Simon asked.

She looked at him consideringly. "Well, I don't know. You tricked me into standing up with you at the assembly."

"Trickery is something you should know about," he said, grinning. "I'm not claiming you owe me a dance, but do grant me this one."

She laughed and curtsied. "Thank you, sir, that will be delightful."

Sir Wilfred came up as she laid her hand on Simon's arm and turned toward the floor. He frowned, obviously disgruntled. In Gerald's absence he had doubtless expected to regain his former precedence, but after all, this was an informal hop not a grand ball. Mimi graciously granted him the second set.

"And after that I'll take my turn to sit out," she said to Simon, who at once resolved that nothing on earth should make him stand up for the third set.

He danced the second with the Marbury cousin, who bounced through the figures with an enthusiasm he enjoyed. As the final chord twanged from the harpsichord close beside them, his gaze at once searched out Mimi.

She came over to invite Mrs. Cooper to take a rest from playing, then signaled to Waring to bring the vicar's wife a glass of wine. With a sparkling smile at Simon, she moved on to make sure that all her guests had their desired refreshment. He watched her stroll about the room, exchanging a few words with Lady Thompson, the squire, the vicar. Her graceful movements had not changed, but she had gained in confidence since the dinner party that had been her first effort as hostess. She was at once gracious and friendly.

He could imagine her at his side, growing with him into the positions of Earl and Countess of Derwent, and later Marquis and Marchioness of Stokesbury.

His imagination removed him in spirit from the drawing room of Salters Hall. When he returned to the present, Mimi had disappeared.

Harriet, already taking to the floor partnered by Mr. Blake, shot Simon a look of desperate appeal. He nodded and slipped out of the room into the entrance hall. Not a sign of her. Recalling the double doors opening from the drawing room into the dining room, he wondered, hopefully, if she might have gone to check on the supper arrangements.

The butler emerged from the dining room as Simon approached.

"Is Miss Lassiter in there, Waring?" he asked.

"No, sir."

Jacko adored Mimi, Simon thought; Cook allowed her to keep tadpoles in a casserole in the scullery; Baird hunted out his late master's effects for her amusement and had shielded her charms from the view of the picnickers. Was it possible that this superior manservant had an equally soft spot for his mistress?

He had to risk it. "I may be making a cake of myself," he said, "but I'm going to ask you to do something for Miss Mimi. I want you to prevent her from entering the drawing room through the dining room, whether you stand out here in the hall or by the double doors."

"Sir?" Waring was understandably startled.

"I'll be waiting outside the drawing-room door," Simon plowed on, feeling an utter mooncalf, "and I can't see how she could slip by me, but she might. Please, for her sake, keep guard with me."

The butler gave him a level stare, then nodded slowly. "Miss Mimi's inclined to be a trifle impetuous," he acknowledged. "I wouldn't want her to come to harm—nor I don't want to know what's afoot, sir," he added hastily, holding up his hand. "Keep her out of the drawing room, you say?"

"Until I've spoken to her."

"Right, sir. I could have a footman watch the other door and fetch you if she comes."

"Good gad, no! I trust your discretion, Waring, but the fewer people know anything about this the better. If I'm right, that is."

"Well, here's hoping you're not, sir," said the butler and padded back into the dining room.

Simon stood by the drawing-room door, a slab of solid Tudor oak that let pass only the faintest sounds of harpsichord, dancing feet, and conversation. A branch of candles stood on a heavy Jacobean table on the far side of the whitewashed hall, barely illuminating the high, open-beamed ceiling. To one side of the table was the door to the library, and next to it the door to the ladies' sitting room.

Mimi could be innocently occupied in either room, but it seemed unlikely. Waring would surely have known if she had gone down the passage beside the staircase to consult Cook about supper. Simon glanced doubtfully at the front door. It was a damp evening—why should she go outside?

No, she must be upstairs. He could think of reasonable explanations, but by now he was almost sure Harriet was right.

A rustle from the top of the stairs alerted him. Mimi stood there, her hand on the newel post. Her face was in shadow, but the rest of her was all too visible.

She was wearing a brief band of silk covering her bosom, and a filmy skirt hung to her ankles from a narrow strip of silk about her hips. A number of gauzy scarves draped her figure, but in the light of the branch of candles on the landing behind her, they were all entirely transparent.

Simon bounded up the stairs. She backed away as he came to a halt just below the top.

"Oh no, Princess," he said. "Oh no." It had been difficult to resist her charms when they were both wet, cold, and shivering after swimming in the mere. It was damnably difficult now, when she stood warmly desirable not an arm's length away, her slender waist, the gentle swell of her hips, the smooth line of her thighs all exposed to his view. Could her skin possibly be as soft as it looked?

Simon blinked and shook his head. He did his best to

make his voice express nothing but sternness. "Go and change at once. I shall be waiting below." He turned and stumped down the stairs.

When he reached the hall, he looked back. She was gone. Releasing Waring from his post, he resumed his by the drawing-room door.

Mimi came down a few minutes later, once more a respectably clad goddess of the southern seas—a subdued goddess who avoided meeting his eyes.

"It really wouldn't have done, Princess," he said softly, opening the door for her. She nodded, still not looking at him, and went past him into the room.

To Simon, Harriet's heartfelt gratitude was no compensation for losing Mimi's confidence.

=17=

THE TADPOLES HAD WELL-DEVELOPED rear legs by now, and the buds of their front legs were showing. Changing their water with Jacko's assistance, Mimi wondered whether Simon would ever come to help her again.

He had looked so stern last night, no hint of laughter in his eyes, no warmth in his peremptory voice. And for the rest of the evening his grave expression had kept her at a distance. How could she have guessed that for once she ought to have heeded Harriet's remonstrances? Simon hadn't cared when she went hatless and gloveless, when she wore a sari and sat on the floor to play the sitar, when she played cricket. English customs were impossible to fathom!

"They'll be wanting a shallower dish soon, miss," Jacko's voice broke into her thoughts, "wi' a bit o' stone to practice climbing out o' the water a ways."

"I'll ask Cook," she said absently. She wanted to be alone to wallow in misery.

"Right, Miss Mimi, and I'll find a nice stone for 'em. 'Tis a fair wonder how they've growed, ain't it?"

She nodded. "Thank you, Jacko. I shan't ride this morning."

Going up to her chamber, she put on gloves and a bonnet, and a lutestring spencer over her cambric walking dress, for it was cloudy and there was a cool breeze blowing. Then she added a parasol in case the sun should come out. She would walk down to the pond. If by chance she met anyone who happened to be riding by, he would have to admit that she was dressed with the utmost respectability.

The gardens were full of the scent of roses. Mimi stopped to bury her nose in the heart of a particularly glorious crimson bloom, but even that rich fragrance failed to cheer her. She passed the borders of delphiniums, pinks, lupins, and irises without a second glance.

At the top of the ha-ha steps she paused. From here she could see over the hedges into the meadows on each side of the paddock—not a horseman in sight.

Disconsolate, she started down the steps. An eager whine from below made her glance down. A small dog, black, white, and tan, was limping toward the foot of the steps, looking up with such hope in its melting brown eyes that she laughed and hurried.

"What, then, have you a thorn in your paw?" she asked.

She sat down on the next-to-bottom step and held out her hand. The dog—he was no more than a puppy, she saw—hesitated a few feet away.

"Come on," Mimi urged, taking off her gloves. "Let me see it. You look like the Pells' foxhounds. Have you run away?"

The bedraggled creature crawled toward her, the very tip of his tail twitching tentatively. As he sniffed at her shoe and then her hand, she noted a cut on his head just above one eye. He was dreadfully thin, his ribs showing through the matted coat.

"You poor little thing. I'll call you Rohan. Because that means sandalwood in Hindi," she explained, wrinkling her nose, "and a bath in sandalwood certainly would not come amiss." She stroked the soft puppy-fur on top of his head and he rolled onto his back, presenting his stomach for petting.

Mimi was horrified. A raw gash cut across the thin flank nearest her, and when she touched Rohan's rib cage he yelped in pain, struggling to his feet. With a humble, apologetic look, he licked her hand and held up his sore paw.

A careful inspection of the muddy limb revealed no thorn in the pads, no obvious injury.

"The Pells must be worrying about you," she told him, recalling the squire's proud description of his best bitch's litter. "They will know how to take care of you. The sooner we get you home, the better."

Carrying Rohan, she set off across the fields. She had never been to the Pells' house since there was no lady in the household, but she knew the way. It was not much more than a mile off. The puppy seemed to put on weight as she walked, and the stiles were difficult to climb until she decided to put him down to creep underneath, which had the added benefit of resting her tired arms.

The last stile faced across a lane to a pair of sagging, rusted gates. Rohan clasped to her chest, Mimi crossed the lane and started up the Pells' narrow drive.

The gravel was pitted with yellowish puddles. On either side, unpruned laurel bushes strangled in a mass of ivy that reached out waving tendrils as she passed. Emerging unscathed, except for one wet shoe and a muddy hem, she paused to look across what must once have been a lawn at a house so buried in ivy she couldn't guess whether it was built of brick or stone.

"Ugh," she said to Rohan, and he licked her chin.

As soon as her feet stopped crunching on the gravel, she heard the distant sound of barking dogs. The drive branched just ahead. The right fork probably led to the kennels, she decided, and turned in that direction. After a few feet the gravel petered out, exposing a veritable mire. She took to the verge, which was at least clean though the long grass was damp. Soon she was wet to the knees.

The dog sounds grew louder. Rohan began to whine as they went around a curve, past screening bushes. A series of fenced enclosures and sheds lay before them, aswarm with yapping, yelping foxhounds.

Mimi had grown quite used to Rohan's smell, but the stink of the kennels assaulted her nostrils. Involuntarily, she stepped back.

A large man carrying a bucket was just latching the gate of one of the runs. He wore a low-crowned hat with a narrow brim, a leather jerkin over a grimy shirt, leather breeches and high boots. Mimi didn't much like the look of him, but he would surely know how to take care of Rohan's injuries.

"I've brought one of your puppies back," she announced. "He's hurt."

The kennelman swung round. "Eh, missy, you did startle me. One o' my pups, you say? Ain't none missing as I knows of. Lessee." He came closer. "Nay, that's our Juno's runt. Won't never make good, that 'un."

"But he's injured. At least you could take care of him till he has healed."

He guffawed. "Bless your tender heart, missy, us had to throw stones at un to drive un off. Ain't nowt to be done wi' the runt o' the litter. Gi' un here," he grunted, reaching out a filthy hand. "I'll drown un this time."

In his frantic scramble to escape, Rohan knocked off Mimi's bonnet before she managed to pin him against her shoulder. Hanging by the ribbons, it dangled down her back.

The man grasped the pup by the loose skin on his shoulders.

"Let go at once!" Mimi ordered.

"Nay, missy, un's no good to man nor beast."

"Let go! How dare you!" She hit his arm with her parasol.

He twisted the parasol from her grasp and broke it across his knee, then stood glaring down at her grimly, hands on hips. "I don't take kindly to females as interferes," he growled. "What Squire does wi' his dogs ain't none o' your affair."

"A hurt animal should be everyone's affair," she berated him, backing away as he reached out again. "I hope you come back as a dog in your next incarnation, a dog with a master as cruel as you are. Or better still, a rat."

"Who you calling a rat!" His reaching hand turned into a fist.

*　*　*

"Gerald! What the devil are you doing here?" Simon demanded as his cousin entered the breakfast parlor.

"My dear fellow, you saw me last night when you returned from tripping the light fantastic at Salters Hall. Coffee, please, Baird, and I shall help myself." He went to the loaded sideboard and peered under silver covers.

"I know you're back from Crossfields, but I own myself astonished to see you at this hour in the morning. Never say you're growing accustomed to country hours at last."

Grinning, Gerald helped himself to kidneys, bacon, and toasted muffins and joined Simon at the table. "I fear I am about to shock you, coz. If you have no definite engagement to Wickham, I shall ride out with you. It is past time you saw the damage a careless landlord can do."

"Squire Pell? Wickham inveighs against him, but he won't take me to see for myself. He says it's unwise to trespass on the squire's land."

Baird, returning with a pot of hot coffee, snorted. "The squire's been known to transport trespassers," he observed. "Sir Josiah, now, was respected for his fairness as justice of the peace. He never made an example of someone he had a personal grudge against."

"I am sure Uncle Josiah was an exemplary magistrate," said Gerald, "but I hardly think even Pell would go so far as to transport my bailiff and Lord Derwent, even in his present guise."

"More like to take a potshot at them," muttered the old man.

"Possibly. Thank you, Baird, that will be all. What I propose, Simon, is to call at the house after riding across his fields. He can hardly take offense because we came in the back way."

"I wager his lordship, Viscount Litton of Crossfields, may approach from any direction he pleases," Simon agreed. "Hurry up with those kidneys, coz, I'm ready to go."

An hour later they were riding down a lane between a farm belonging to Mere House and one of the Pells' tenants. Gerald pointed out the weed-choked ditches on the squire's side, the gaps in the hedge where bushes and trees had died and not been replaced. Coming to a rickety gate, they turned into a plowed field.

"Winter wheat," said Simon, judging the crop by its near readiness for harvest. "But why is it only planted down the sides of the field, except for those few clumps in the middle?"

"You used to ride to hounds before you took to chasing Frenchies across the waves."

"You mean the hunt crossed here? I suppose a few dozen galloping horses at the wrong time could cause such devastation, but I'm surprised it hasn't been replanted."

"Replanting costs money. Pell may have paid compensation, but either it was insufficient or his overseer pocketed some portion of it."

They rode on, across soggy, undrained meadows grazed by cattle mired to their knees; through woodland where dead trees rotted in the underbrush; past a farmhouse with cracked windows and tottering chimney, and unsmiling, unshod children in the littered yard.

"Can nothing be done?" Simon asked, appalled.

"They are Pell's acres and Pell's tenants. I know Uncle Josiah tried to reason with him without success. It would cost a fortune now to put all to rights."

"Mimi's fortune."

"I doubt it would be spent that way if Albert could get his hands on it, which I also doubt. The colonel is aware of the state of the squire's land."

"I hope he's seen it for himself. I'd heard enough stories, but without actually setting eyes on it I couldn't really imagine it. Gerald, I'm going to insist that my father let me manage our estates. I cannot bear to think that our tenants might be living in such conditions."

"Nothing as bad as this, I believe. Your agents are too well paid to risk their positions by gross negligence or by dishonesty. But nothing is done quite as well as it could be."

"What I don't understand is why the devil didn't Cedric make more effort to take over the reins. Was he unaware of the problems? You must have pointed them out to him."

"I did, on more than one occasion."

"Surely he wasn't afraid of losing my father's regard? I don't believe anything he could have done would have damned him in the marquis's eyes."

Instead of answering, Gerald drew rein and gestured at the house that now stood before them. Absorbed in their discussion, Simon hadn't noticed the ivy-clad manor, merging as it did into the overgrown shrubbery surrounding it. Windows peered like eyes beneath shaggy brows, and the terrace sported a beard of grass.

"The devil!" said Simon. "The Pells live no better than their tenants."

"Not much. All they care for is sport. Simon, your father ordered me not to tell you about Cedric, but half the world knows and I cannot in good conscience keep you in ignorance."

"What is there to know, other than that he was a buck of the first stare, a model of fashionable elegance, a superb sportsman, the handsome darling of the *ton*, in short perfection itself? Everything a gentleman could want in his son and heir." Simon tried, without a great deal of success, to keep the bitterness from his voice.

"He was also a libertine who cared not whom he cuckolded, nor what innocence he destroyed," said Gerald brutally. "He was a gamester who would have bankrupted the family but for the luck that enabled him to ruin several others instead. He never lost his welcome in polite society, but he preferred to frequent the coarsest scoundrels and he died in a drunken brawl in a low tavern."

"But . . . but why . . ." Simon stammered. He read honesty in his cousin's eyes, and loyalty and—was it confident hope? "I was told Cedric was killed in a carriage accident."

Gerald set his horse in motion and Simon automatically followed suit. "Your parents are still trying to pretend it never happened. They prefer the myth of perfection to the truth, and against that myth you can never win. To my mind, you are worth a dozen of your brother, and I am proud . . . What the devil!"

Even Simon's preoccupation vanished at the sight that met their eyes as they rounded a stand of elms. A man in the clothes of an outdoor servant advanced with upraised fist on a slim figure who faced him defiantly, shielding something in her arms.

"Mimi!" cried Simon, urging Intrepid to a gallop, Gerald's mount matching every stride.

As the two horses thundered down upon him, the fellow backed off, then turned tail and ran. Mimi stood her ground until she recognized them. At once she set her burden on the ground and began to struggle with her bonnet, hanging down her back.

Intrepid slowed and stopped. Simon dismounted and went to help with the recalcitrant bonnet.

"The brim is torn," he told her, straightening it, "and I fear one of the roses will never be the same again. You're hard on hats, Miss Lassiter."

"You are thinking of the one I threw in the mere. That horrid man broke my parasol," she added, looking mournfully at the sad remains on the ground, "and I must have left my gloves by the pond. Oh dear, and my spencer is covered with mud and blood and dog hairs."

"Blood! Oh, from the dog," he said in relief as she stooped to pick up the puppy cringing at her feet.

"And my hem is filthy and I stepped in a puddle," she continued the catalog of disaster, "but I'm very glad you came, all the same. Rohan is much heavier than he looks. I'd much rather not have to carry him home again."

"Simon, help Miss Lassiter up behind me," suggested Gerald, his voice full of laughter. "You may have the honor of bearing her mongrel."

"Don't call him a mongrel, coz," Simon advised, seeing Mimi's indignation as he lifted her onto the horse's back. "He's a canine of uncertain parentage."

"He's not! He's a foxhound. That's why I brought him

to the Pells—I was sure he had run away. But they didn't want him, so they threw stones at him to make him leave, and that *odious* man said he'd drown him this time!" She put one arm around Gerald's waist.

Envying his cousin, fearful of what might have happened had they not ridden this way, Simon took the pup from the clasp of her other arm, handling the shivering little body gently. "We'll soon put you to rights, old fellow," he assured him, then looked up at Mimi. She smiled. He was in favor with her again, but it had to be said: "Miss Lassiter, you ought not to have come here alone."

"I know," she said guiltily. "I was in such a hurry to bring Rohan home to be healed that I didn't think about propriety."

"Propriety be damned! It's danger I'm talking about. What do you think that fellow was—"

"Do climb down off your high ropes, coz," Gerald interrupted, "and climb into the saddle, if you can manage it with—er—Rohan in your arms. The sooner we are on our way, the better."

Simon had to acknowledge the sense of this. Mimi was in no condition to come face-to-face with the Pells. Intrepid's good manners allowed him to mount with a minimum of awkwardness, and they set out cross-country for Salters Hall.

In view of Mimi's insecure seat, they rode slowly. Unsure if he was in her black books, Simon kept his mouth shut. She was silent too, whether burning with indignation toward him or consumed with guilt. The cawing of rooks in the elms sounded loud behind them.

Gerald made no effort to break the silence until they left the squire's land, when he inquired, "I take it, Miss Lassiter, that your new pet is not named for the Prince de Rohan, the French cardinal?"

"No, I've never heard of him. Who is he?"

"Wasn't he the one who was involved in the Diamond Necklace scandal?" Simon asked. "Something to do with the French court shortly before the Revolution?"

"Yes," said Gerald shortly and repressively.

Simon gathered that the affair was too unsavory to be discussed in the presence of a young lady. He could tell that a question was rising to Mimi's lips. "I wager Rohan is an Indian name," he said quickly.

"Hindi for sandalwood." She giggled. "You see, when I found him he was rather smelly, so I told him he needed a bath with sandalwood essence."

"Believe me," said Simon, "the name has done absolutely nothing to sweeten his smell."

Rohan's protesting yip at this slander snapped the last thread of tension, and suddenly they were all laughing uproariously.

=18=

"Jacko will look after Rohan while we're at the Daumiers', Papa," said Mimi persuasively.

"And while we're inside Highbury Manor," her father commanded. "He's not house-trained yet."

"He's only a baby. He's going to be excessively handsome when he has put on a bit more weight, is he not?"

"Excessively." The colonel scratched the head of the little dog in his daughter's arms. Rohan wriggled with joy, his tail beating against Mimi's side. "All right, you may bring him. I hope he's carriage-trained at least."

"We can stop halfway and I'll walk him a bit. Harriet and Mr. Cooper won't mind."

"The carriage is at the door, sir," announced Waring.

As he handed Mimi into the carriage, Colonel Lassiter said firmly, "Now none of your tricks today, missy. Lord Daumier has approved my turning the manor into an orphanage, but everything will go much smoother if we're on friendly terms with him and his lady. They're the biggest landowners in the parish of Highbury, and they could make things very awkward if you set up their backs."

"Tricks, Papa?" Mimi looked up at him wide-eyed as she smoothed her skirts and settled Rohan on the soft leather seat beside her.

"Naughty puss," he chuckled, patting her cheek and sitting down opposite her. "Promise me."

"No tricks, Papa. I shall keep on my gloves and my hat and not talk about tadpoles or Indian gods."

"And you won't cut the Pells?"

"Oh dear, are they going too? It will be difficult to be polite after what they let that man do to Rohan, but I promise to try."

"Good enough, my love. There is, thank heaven, no lake for you to fall in. Stay away from the stream."

It was a sunny, windy morning. Rohan pressed his nose to the window for a few minutes, but his breath steamed it up so he gave up trying to see out. He fell asleep with his head on Mimi's lap, only to awaken the moment the carriage stopped outside the vicarage.

Jacko jumped down from the back and ran up the path between beds of scarlet geraniums to knock on the door. The vicar and Harriet came straight out and joined the Lassiters in the carriage. Having already met Harriet, Rohan greeted her with boundless enthusiasm. Mr. Cooper was a stranger, however, and therefore worthy of suspicion. As the carriage rolled through the village, its course was punctuated by short, sharp, questioning barks.

"You ought to know better than to mistrust a clergyman," the vicar told him with mock severity. "Well, Colonel, who is to join us this morning, besides Lord and Lady Daumier?"

"Lady Thompson, of course. I don't know if Lord Litton or Mr. Hurst will come."

"My daughter tells me Lord Litton has expressed an interest in the orphanage, so I daresay he will be there."

Mimi noted Harriet's blush and squeezed her hand. "I wonder why a Pink of the *Ton* should be interested in an orphanage?" she whispered slyly. "For the same reason he came back to Cheshire so unexpectedly?"

"Pell said he'd come by to look the place over," her father continued, "and the Marburys . . ."

"The Marburys?" said the vicar in surprise. "I had not thought any of them seriously interested."

"It's my belief they are only interested in meeting with the Daumiers," the colonel said cynically. "An invitation to take luncheon with them is not to be missed. Lloyd will be there, as vicar of Highbury, and Blake should be there to meet us with the keys. He handled the convey-ancing, as you know. That's all, I think."

"A goodly crowd, yet few enough for that vast house. There has not been even a caretaker there these many years. We had best walk with caution."

"The structure is sound enough in the newer parts, Vicar, but you are right. I'll warn everyone to be careful, especially in the old wing that was the original house."

"Why has the manor been abandoned for so long, Papa?" Mimi asked.

"The last owner—or, rather, resident owner—had only one child, a daughter, who married a colonist and went to America. When he died she couldn't be found, I gather. It was only when she, in turn, died that her son found mention of Highbury Manor among her papers. He contacted an English lawyer and discovered that he now owned the place, which is of no use to him whatso-ever. It's because he's in America that it's taken so long to close the purchase."

After a brief stop for Rohan's sake, they reached High-bury shortly before noon. The manor was visible from a distance across unkempt parkland, a huge, rambling place with sections in every style from early Tudor to modern Palladian.

"It's perfect for an orphanage," Mimi said as they drove up the avenue of chestnuts. "There's space enough for dozens of children. What's that turret on the roof, Papa?"

"Blake said it's a banqueting room, though it hardly looks big enough to hold a banquet in."

"In Tudor times, and well into the seventeenth cen-tury," the vicar explained, "a banquet could be a grand feast or a light refreshment for a few friends. The Eliza-bethans often built small, elaborate buildings for the lat-ter purpose in the gardens, but the roof was also a popular location. I see you have gardeners at work al-ready, Colonel."

"Yes, the gardens are so impenetrable it's impossible even to see what needs to be done. When they've been cleared a bit, I shall want Mrs. Cooper's advice. She, if anyone, must know how to create a garden that won't be ruined by children's games."

"Sir," said Harriet shyly, "I believe I can tell you what Mama would advise."

The colonel smiled at her. "Tell me."

"If you allow the children to help in the garden, let them plant things, and pick the flowers and vegetables, then they will be careful not to spoil it because they will feel it belongs to them."

The vicar nodded approvingly, and the colonel said, "An excellent point, Miss Harriet. I can see your opinion is going to be valuable, and I hope you won't stint to express it. Well, here we are. Blake is before us, it seems."

The front door of the manor, beneath an impressive portico sadly in need of paint, stood open. They found the lawyer and Mr. Lloyd within, and the Marburys and Squire Pell arrived not long after. Next came Lord and Lady Daumier, a distinguished middle-aged couple dressed with a quiet elegance greatly at odds with the frills and furbelows of the fawning Marburys.

"Lady Daumier makes Lady Marbury look like an opera dancer," Mimi whispered to Harriet.

"Oh, Mimi, how do you know what an opera dancer looks like?" asked Harriet, whose sailor-brother Ferdie had enlightened her on the subject of Fashionable Impures.

"We went to the Royal Opera House when we were in London, before we came here," her friend explained innocently. "The dancers wore excessively ornate costumes. Lady Daumier's dress is much simpler, but it looks much smarter, does it not?"

"Much. If I were rich, I should endeavor to copy her style. Listen, do you hear another carriage?"

"It must be Lady Thompson. Let's go and see if Simon and Gerald are with her."

"Oh no, we ought not . . . ," Harriet chuckled, " . . . but as hostess you might go out to welcome her."

With a most unladylike snort, Mimi caught her arm and pulled her out to the portico.

Lady Thompson was accompanied by both her young relatives, Gerald in the carriage with her, Simon riding alongside.

"Come in," Mimi invited gaily. "Lord and Lady Daumier are here already, everyone's here, and Papa is ready to conduct a tour." She ushered Lady Thompson into the dingy marble hall.

Following, Harriet noticed that Lord Litton appeared amused. He murmured something in Simon's ear which brought a look of alarm to Simon's face. Then they were inside, in the now crowded hall, in a confusion of greetings.

Lady Thompson, a longtime neighbor, knew the Daumiers well if not intimately, and Gerald was acquainted with them from London Society. Harriet was surprised when Simon was not presented to them. She looked around for him, but forgot all about him when Gerald joined her.

"The colonel wishes every lady to have an escort," he said. "He has offered my aunt his arm, so may I have the pleasure of offering you mine?"

Speechless with pleasure, Harriet laid her hand in the crook of his arm and they followed Colonel Lassiter and his motley crowd of advisers.

The house was, as Squire Pell loudly and repeatedly described it, "a demmed rabbit warren." Inside as out, no effort had been made to merge the various additions into a harmonious whole. Doors in odd places led from fancifully baroque drawing rooms into plain, wainscoted Jacobean parlors.

"The first thing I'll do," said the colonel, "is put in proper connecting passageways."

"Oh no," Harriet said, involuntarily but softly.

"No?" Gerald smiled down at her, his eyebrows raised.

"I like it the way it is. You never know what you will come upon next. But more important, I think the children will be happier in small groups, more like a proper family, than all thrown together in an indistinguishable mass. If there are few connections between the parts of the house, each will be more like a home."

"You are undoubtedly right. Tell the colonel."

"I could not! Later, when there are not so many people."

"They will not bite you, you know. And if you leave it till later, Colonel Lassiter will have started to build plans on a faulty foundation. Courage, Miss Harriet." Covering her hand with his, he raised his voice. "Colonel, this young lady has a suggestion to make."

Everyone stopped and turned and looked at her. Harriet was ready to sink—or would have been without the encouragement of Gerald's hand gently pressing hers.

"Good," said the colonel. "Miss Cooper has already made one valuable suggestion."

So she told them her ideas, which were greeted with thoughtful murmurs and nods of approval. The tour continued.

"You see?" said Gerald. "That was not so dreadful, was it? Shakespeare wrote something about the foolishness of hiding one's light under a bushel. Or is it in the Bible?"

"In the Bible."

"Is it not amazing how most quotations, and a great many common sayings, are in the Bible or from Shakespeare?"

Her composure restored, Harriet agreed with a smile. They followed the others into a long Elizabethan gallery with windows on one side overlooking the gardens. The opposite wall was hung with portraits so cobwebbed they might all have been of the same person. The portraits should be cleaned and kept, Harriet told Gerald, so that the children could pretend they were of their own ancestors.

"I shall tell the colonel later," she said firmly. "It cannot make any difference to . . ."

"Colonel, sir!" A panting youth in soil-stained clothes rushed into the gallery, clutching a pair of shears. "Sir, I bin sent to tell 'ee there's a female on the roof!"

Harriet was not in the least surprised to discover that Mimi was missing.

As they followed Mimi and Aunt Georgina into the hall of Highbury Manor, Gerald had murmured in Simon's ear, "I was not aware that the Daumiers were to be here. You met them once in town, and your father was closely associated with Lord Daumier two or three years ago in sponsoring some bill in the Lords."

Simon shuddered and hung back. The last thing he wanted was to be exposed before the entire neighborhood. He was ready to flee, but Mimi, having handed his aunt over to the colonel, came up to him.

"Papa means to show everyone the whole musty old house, but I doubt they will get so far as the banqueting room, right at the top, that I want to see. Papa says every lady must have a gentleman's escort. Will you come with me?"

"Certainly. Let's escape at once before we're trapped."

They hurried up the nearest stairs, then headed in the direction of the older part of the manor. The rooms they glanced into, dimly lit by curtained windows, were all full of the lurking shapes of furniture in dusty holland covers. Their footsteps, muffled by dust, were the only sound until a floorboard creaked loudly as they passed. Mimi grabbed Simon's hand and hung on.

Proceeding ever upward, they found at last a winding stair that looked promising. At the top a small door in a turret opened directly onto a flat area of roof, enclosed by a stone parapet.

"There it is," Mimi said with great satisfaction and started eagerly toward a belvedere some thirty feet off.

"Wait. We don't know what condition the leads are in. Let me go first."

"Leads?"

"That's what a roof walk is called, I suppose because the roof is made of lead." Simon repressed the temptation to tell her of the forays he and Gerald had made onto the roofs of his Hampshire home, the historic battles refought among chimney pots and gables. Cedric had considered them childish. What had made Cedric take the wrong turning that had led to his death in a tavern brawl?

Dismissing the question, he went cautiously forward across the roof, holding Mimi's hand to stop her from moving ahead. The gusty wind was strong up here, buffeting them playfully, but the roof seemed sound. They reached the banqueting room without any difficulty.

The turret was no more than a dozen feet square, with a pillar in each corner, arched windows, and a domed roof. The door, in the side nearest to them, was locked with a huge, ornate, rusty but still sound iron lock.

"Botheration!" said Mimi. "I wanted to see the view."

"You can see it even better from out here," Simon pointed out, laughing. "Those windows are filthy. Look, if we climb that slope, the chimney stack will shelter us from the wind. Let's sit down there and you can admire the view to your heart's content."

He helped her up the pitched roof and they sat with their backs to the sun-warmed brick. The rich green fields of Cheshire, dotted with cows, stretched before them, merging into the hills of Derbyshire and Staffordshire.

"It's so very different from Bharadupatam. Most of the time, when you looked out from the highest tower in my grandfather's palace everything was brown as far as you could see. Even the trees were dust-brown except in the monsoons. England is very beautiful." She sighed.

"You have found it difficult to adjust to English life, I think," he said gently. "I can guess a little of what you have gone through, for the change from the freedom of the seas to the constrictions of a landlubber has not been easy for me."

"For me it's been the other way about. Oh, when I was a child I used to go everywhere with Papa, to the villages and bazaars and temples and barracks. But when I was eleven my grandfather insisted that I must go into purdah. You know what that is? A woman must never be seen by a strange man, so you live behind curtains and behind walls. If I went out, it was in a palanquin with more curtains, and stifling veils to hide my face in case the curtains blew open. I hardly ever saw Papa anymore, because if he came to visit me everyone else had to hide."

"And your mother?"

"She died when I was eight. I don't really remember

her, except that she was beautiful and had the softest voice."

Simon took her hand for comfort. She was wearing thin cotton gloves, and as he held her slender fingers he realized he ought not to have brought her up here alone. He didn't give a damn.

Mimi went on. "Mrs. Forbes came to teach me about England. That is, to teach me the things an English young lady learns, but what I liked best were the stories about England. I used to dream about driving through Hyde Park in an open carriage, and going into shops to buy things, and talking to young men—even dancing with them! England seemed a paradise of freedom."

However luxurious her grandfather's palace, he thought, she had been little better than a prisoner. No wonder she shied from a kiss! When speaking to a young man was forbidden, a stolen kiss became virtually equivalent to seduction.

"And then you came here?" he prompted.

"It *was* a paradise. For months I felt free as a bird. Oh, Mrs. Forbes had taught me all the rules, but compared to purdah they were nothing. But then I started to think, if the rules of purdah could be rejected so easily, what made the English conventions different? Some of them were obviously silly. As I said to Harriet, why should I wear a bonnet to protect my complexion when my skin is brown anyway?"

"What did Harriet say to that?"

"She had no answer. There is no answer. It's all so confusing. Some people are upset if I don't wear a hat and some people don't care. How can I possibly guess what will simply vex a few prim old ladies and what is truly scandalous?"

Simon wanted to hold her tight and tell her not to worry, all she had to do was to entrust herself to him for the rest of her life and he would smooth her path. He would stop her dancing half naked—in company, at least—but as far as he was concerned he didn't mind if she never wore a hat again.

Then he realized that he did mind. As his countess, his marchioness one day, she would have to conform to certain conventions, however senseless, or be ostracized by the society to which he wanted to present her proudly.

"As a sailor," he said slowly, "I find many of the rules of etiquette silly. Nonetheless, in the end life is easier if one obeys them. I'm not saying that you shouldn't keep tadpoles, only that if you invite your guests to see them you are bound to offend some. Take off your bonnet when you walk alone in the garden, but wear it to the village. And some of the rules are for your safety. . . ."

"Mimi!" The colonel appeared in the doorway to the stair turret. "My dear girl!" He ventured out, followed by Squire Pell and Lord Daumier.

"View halloo!" bellowed the squire.

Simon stood up, helped Mimi to her feet, and steadied her down the brief slope to the leads. "We have just been admiring the view," he murmured to her.

She nodded. "Hallo, Papa," she said composedly. "Mr. Hurst was kind enough to bring me up here to see the banqueting room, but it is locked. We stayed for a few minutes to admire the view."

"A superb view," agreed Lord Daumier. "There is my house, and I believe I can see the Welsh mountains to the west." He turned back to the turret. "My dear, a most pleasant roof walk, though a trifle windy. Do you care to come out?"

Lady Daumier stepped over the sill. "Delightful. How clever of you to find it, Miss Lassiter." She looked at Simon in a puzzled way.

"Blake," called the colonel, "have you the key to the banqueting room?"

The lawyer joined them, and then Gerald and Harriet. Simon slipped round behind the growing crowd, trying to keep out of sight of the Daumiers. He shouldn't have let Henry practice his skills on his old clothes.

"I'm off," he muttered to Gerald, "before her ladyship recalls where she's seen me before."

As he started down the stairs he heard the colonel ask, "Where's Hurst?"

"He went to inform my aunt that all is well," came Gerald's smooth reply.

The Daumiers might connect Simon's surname with his father's and think it odd, but Simon doubted that in his absence they would mention it. He found Aunt Georgina and the rest of the party, reassured them, and hastily departed.

"I don't know what to think," Mimi confided to Rohan as she settled him in his stable bed for the night. "Be good now. You'll soon be housebroken and then you can sleep in my chamber. You see," she continued, "once Lady Daumier had so kindly made it seem unexceptionable to be on the roof, Simon might have decided that if he disappeared people would forget we'd been up there alone together."

Rohan uttered a drowsy bark and licked her hand.

"That's what you think, is it? Only if so, why did he go home, not wait downstairs? I have a lowering feeling that he suddenly realized, when they all arrived, how improper it was for us to be alone together. The female is always blamed for such transgressions, Mrs. Forbes says. Do you think Simon is angry with me again?"

The puppy's adoring brown eyes assured her that no one could possibly ever be angry with her, but she was not convinced.

=19=

"PAPA, MR. LLOYD HAS just proposed to me."

The colonel set down on his desk the orphanage plans he was studying. The corners of his eyes crinkled with amusement as he surveyed his puzzled daughter. "You refused him, I take it, as you did the others?"

"Yes, Sir Wilfred on Monday and Albert Pell yesterday." Mimi shifted a pile of papers and perched on the corner of the desk. "Do you think Mr. Blake will come tomorrow?"

"Very likely. I daresay business has kept him from rushing to your side. Do you mean to reject him, too?" He smiled at her emphatic nod. "Since you care for none of them, I'll explain why they are all coming up to scratch at once. You see, my dear, it took none of them long after our arrival here to discover that you are a wealthy young lady. With varying degrees of discretion, they all waited a decent interval before approaching me to ask for your hand in marriage."

"Just long enough to make it seem they might have developed a *tendre* for me?" Given her low opinion of those concerned, Mimi was neither surprised nor chagrined.

"Precisely. I told them, one and all, that you must have time to become accustomed to English Society before you chose a husband, and I set a period of one year from our arrival."

"Which expired just the other day." She laughed. "And

to think I thought it was because I have behaved with such decorum for a whole week! Well, I must be off. Mr. Blake has made me late fetching Harriet for our ride, and Lady Thompson is expecting us." Leaning across the desk, she kissed his cheek. "Thank you, Papa, for making them wait. A year ago I should not have known how to handle them at all."

She went to change into her riding habit, then she and Jacko rode down to the vicarage, Rohan trotting alongside well clear of the horses' hooves. Approaching the house, she saw Mr. Lloyd riding off toward the village, his shoulders slumped disconsolately. She stared after him, a fascinating surmise bringing a grin to her face.

As soon as Harriet, with Jacko's help, was mounted on Shridatta, Mimi demanded, "Has Mr. Lloyd just offered for your hand?"

"Well, yes . . . but, Mimi, one ought not to discuss a gentleman's proposal."

"You can tell me. I won't tell anyone."

"How did you guess?"

"I saw him riding away from the vicarage looking glum, and as I rejected him in no uncertain terms not an hour since . . ."

"You put two and one together and came up with four." Smiling, Harriet shook her head. "Your logic defies me, but you are right."

"And have Albert Pell and Sir Wilfred also proposed this week?"

"Mr. Pell, yes. Not Sir Wilfred."

"Oh well, he is going to London in the autumn. I daresay he is hoping for bigger game. I prophesy that Lawyer Blake will be on your doorstep for the same purpose in a day or two."

"I am willing to believe you, but why?"

Mimi explained how her father had forbidden her suitors to approach her for a year. "So I thought, since I had turned them off they might well come straight to you," she finished.

"The colonel's postponement was fortunate for me,"

Harriet said. "A year ago I should have accepted an offer. I cannot imagine how I could have thought I might be happy married to any of them."

"It's only three months since I set about my plan to return them to you."

Jacko opened the meadow gate and they rode through. Mimi was silent, pondering all that had happened in those three months. She halted Deva Lal when they reached the paddock and sat looking at the pond. If it hadn't been for the gadflies around the pond last summer, she'd never have gone fishing for tadpoles in the mere and her meeting with Simon would have taken a quite different course. She sighed.

Harriet echoed her sigh. "Now I know what a true gentleman is like," she murmured. "I could not marry anyone else. Yet it is near a fortnight since he returned from Crossfields, and he has not spoken."

"How impatient you are! I'm sure lords have to consider such an important step with the utmost care. He will marry you in the end."

"Do you really think so? Recently it seems to me he has paid you as much attention as he has me."

"He has been unusually affable, no doubt because I've been on my best behavior. I'm beginning to quite like him, but don't worry, Harriet, I shan't have him even if he does propose."

"I don't want him to propose to you!" Harriet wailed.

Rohan, sprawling exhausted on the grass, sat up and barked in sympathy. Startled, Shridatta tossed her head, distracting Harriet from her woes—fortunately, as Mimi had no ready answer.

"Jacko, hand Rohan to me, please," she said. "He's too little to run all the way. Come on, Lady Thompson will be wondering where we are."

Baird admitted them to Mere House. He gave Rohan, in Mimi's arms, a benevolent pat.

"So this is the young fellow you rescued, miss. A taking little chap. I understand the Reverend Lloyd called at Salters Hall this afternoon?" He winked.

"How on earth did you know that already?"

"Now that would be telling, miss. Three down and one to go, eh? This way, if you please, ladies. Her ladyship is expecting you."

Mimi was more surprised by the speed of the butler's knowledge than by the fact that he knew of her suitors' coming up to scratch. She was not at all surprised by Lady Thompson's greeting.

"So, Mimi, my dear, Baird tells me you have turned down three offers in as many days."

"Yes, ma'am. But Harriet says it is wrong to speak of it."

"Very proper. You will not wish to embarrass the gentlemen whose suit you have dismissed. However, those of us not personally involved are free to speculate to our hearts' content and to tease you about it. You mean to reject Blake, too, I trust?"

"My lips are sealed," said Mimi virtuously, taking a seat beside Harriet on a small sofa.

"I daresay your papa warned you that they are all fortune hunters. Sir Wilfred is well enough to pass, of course, but the Marburys would like to enter the Fashionable World. I was never so surprised in my life as when that woman told Lady Daumier they are all to go to Town for the Little Season."

"Sophia was crowing odiously." Mimi giggled. "I could not but be glad when Lady Daumier said they rarely spend much time in London in the autumn."

"She said it in such a kind way," Harriet put in, "as if she was sorry she could not invite the Marburys to call."

"You may be sure she was relieved," said Lady Thompson firmly. "Who would choose to have about them such toad-eaters as the Marburys? Would you believe that woman came next to me to try for introductions to some of my friends!"

"Have you tonnish friends, ma'am?" Mimi asked. "I did not know."

"I had my Season before I married Sir Josiah, and he and I were used to go sometimes to town. I have kept up a correspondence with several *grandes dames* of Society, though I have seen little of them of late. I hope I know better than to inflict that Marbury woman and her spiteful daughter upon them."

Harriet was obviously uncomfortable with this uncharitable conversation, so Mimi changed the subject. "Tell us about your Season, ma'am. I daresay things were very different then."

"To be sure. It was before the French Revolution, you know, which made such a change to our manners and fashions though it never spread to England, heaven be praised."

Baird brought in the tea just then. Absently nibbling on macaroon after macaroon, her ladyship described gowns of heavy velvet and brocade over hooped petticoats so wide a lady had to pass through a door sideways; face patches with names like the Adorable and the Kissing, and hair piled high over horsehair pads; gentlemen in powdered wigs, with high-heeled shoes and clocked stockings, who always wore swords and challenged each other to duels at the drop of a gold-laced tricorne hat.

Mimi listened with one ear, having heard much the same from Mrs. Forbes. The other ear was alert for any indication that Simon and Gerald were coming to join them. She was taken by surprise when Lady Thompson suddenly stopped in the middle of her reminiscences, held up her hand, and announced in a portentous voice, "I have a splendid notion. In fact, I will go so far as to say I have a plan."

"Oh good." Mimi clapped her hands. "I love plans."

"What is it, ma'am?" Harriet asked cautiously.

"I shall take you both to London for the Season." Ignoring their astounded gasps, she continued, "With your money, Mimi, and my connections, we shall all have a grand time. And you will both meet dozens, nay, scores of eligible gentlemen and make splendid matches and show those country bumpkin fortune hunters who have been pursuing you so assiduously, Mimi, and have behaved so disgracefully to you, Harriet, just how insignificant they are." Ending on this triumphant and slightly breathless note, she beamed at them.

Pros and cons raced through Mimi's mind. Harriet already knew whom she wanted to marry, but an announcement of his aunt's plan might serve to prod Lord Litton into action. If not, the rivals for Harriet's hand to be found in London might turn the trick. At worst, the entertainments of town could serve to distract her from her disappointment. She might even find someone else she liked as well as the viscount.

As for herself, Mimi suddenly realized that if she couldn't marry Simon her only choice would be to dwindle into a rich and eccentric old maid. All the talk of fortune hunters had made her realize his difficulty—his pride would rebel at being classified with Albert Pell and Lawyer Blake. She could only hope that he loved her enough to overcome his pride.

She wasn't sure he loved her at all.

Still, if he did, Lady Thompson's plan might persuade him, as well as Gerald Litton, to act. And if he didn't, at least Mimi would be an old maid with memories of the gaiety of a London Season. On the whole, she approved.

She was about to say so when Harriet broke the thoughtful silence.

"It is excessively kind in you to invite me, my lady, but I fear Papa could not possibly bear the expenses of a Season."

"Fustian!" said Mimi. "You cannot suppose that I should enjoy myself in town without your company. Indeed, ma'am, I don't mean that I shall not have need of your support, but tell Harriet how much more comfortable it will be to have a friend of my own age as well."

"Quite right, my dear. Nothing is so fortifying to the spirits as an intimate friend with whom to face the world. So you think the colonel will agree to my plan, Mimi?"

"Oh yes, I have only to say that I want to go."

Harriet's hand in its darned glove smoothed her faded blue cambric skirts. "But I cannot accept—" she began.

"I have a plan!" Mimi interrupted, then added, giving

credit where credit was due, "Or at least a sort of subplan of your plan, ma'am. Harriet, if you don't marry you will have to seek a position as companion or governess, will you not? I shall ask Papa to hire you as my companion. He will understand that you have to have gowns and everything as good as mine, so that people don't think me vain or parsimonious. Please say you will come. I don't believe I am brave enough to face the *ton* without you."

"Remember what a sensation the two of you were at the Chester assembly," Lady Thompson urged.

Her lips quivering, Harriet managed a smile. "I shall have to talk to Papa and Mama."

Mimi hugged her friend. She doubted that Harriet had considered the possibilities of the plan, so obvious to her own fertile imagination. It was probably better not to suggest that Gerald might be encouraged to offer, in case he wasn't.

Looking up, Mimi caught Lady Thompson's speculative gaze on the two of them. Was it possible that she guessed their feelings for her nephews, that her hopes for her plan matched Mimi's?

"Pray ring the bell, Mimi," said her ladyship blandly. "The tea grows cold and all the macaroons have vanished."

"I do believe Mimi Lassiter is quite the most generous girl it has ever been my fortune to know," Lady Thompson announced, accepting Baird's offer of a large slice of rhubarb-and-strawberry pie and pouring thick cream over it.

"Perhaps, never having lacked money, she does not comprehend its value," Gerald suggested. "In many ways she is an innocent, guileless child."

"Hardly guileless," snorted Simon, who did not care to hear his princess praised by the cousin he was fast coming to regard as a rival. "Her endless plots and plans reveal a distinctly Machiavellian cunning."

Gerald grinned. "You must admit she is innocent of

any regard for the consequences. She is at once ingenious and ingenuous."

"As I was about to say," their aunt interrupted firmly, "I am not speaking of monetary generosity alone. Mimi is always eager to make Harriet feel she is doing a favor by accepting a gift, and she sincerely wants Harriet to have the best. I have known many a young lady in my time who was all too glad to have her companions less well dressed than herself."

"Miss Lassiter possesses true generosity of spirit," Gerald admitted.

Simon glared at him, and was taken aback by his aunt's badly hidden amusement. He couldn't believe Aunt Georgina actually enjoyed seeing her nephews at odds.

"To what do we owe this sudden spate of praise for Miss Lassiter, ma'am?" he inquired.

"Why, I have been following her example, Simon. I have been plotting and planning. It is my intention to take Mimi and Harriet up to London for the Little Season at least, possibly in the spring also. It will be vastly entertaining to see the pair of them with suitors swarming about them, as I don't doubt will be the case. Besides, it is an age since I was in town, and I look forward to becoming reacquainted with a number of good friends."

Both Gerald and Simon frowned.

"Miss Cooper cannot possibly afford a Season, Aunt," Gerald pointed out.

"I am well aware of that. Mimi proposes to hire Harriet as her companion. She swears she is too timid to face the *ton* alone."

"Mimi timid!" Simon laughed. "I can't imagine her abashed by even the most redoubtable of dowagers. She stood up to Pell's bullying kennelman with nary a blink."

"She is pluck to the backbone," Gerald concurred, "though I had rather face a dozen kennelmen than any one of some dowagers I am acquainted with. Have both young ladies accepted your invitation, Aunt Georgina?"

"Of course. Did you imagine either would turn down such an opportunity?" Lady Thompson finished her last mouthful of pie and rose to her feet. "Now do not sit too long over your port, pray," she said, and swept out with a self-satisfied expression on her plump face.

Under Baird's direction, two footmen cleared the dishes from the table. The butler set out decanters of port and brandy.

"Will there be anything else, my lord?"

"Thank you, no, unless you can tell me what has put this notion into her ladyship's head."

"I'm sure I can't say, my lord," said Baird with an air of conscious rectitude. He bowed and departed.

"Won't say, more like," Simon grunted. "Aunt Georgina can't afford a Season any better than Harriet Cooper, can she? Do you suppose she expects the colonel to pay her expenses too?"

"Probably. I shall frank her, of course, if it comes to the point, but I doubt that it will. I shall speak to Miss Lassiter tomorrow."

Simon poured himself a large brandy. So his suspicions were justified; his cousin meant to offer for Mimi. He could ride to Salters Hall now, tell her who he really was, beg her to marry him—but then he would never know whether she loved him for himself or for his title.

No, he would have to risk Gerald's succeeding. He was sure Mimi didn't love the viscount, so if she accepted him it would be only because he was a viscount. In that case she was not the girl he had fallen in love with, and losing her would not be quite so dreadful.

He hoped.

The next morning he watched from a window as Gerald rode off under a pall of gray clouds. Was he crackbrained not to spike his guns by going with him? He sat down to read a book Wickham had recommended, but it was impossible to concentrate. Every few lines he found himself listening for Gerald's return. Giving up, he wandered restlessly about the house until he could stand the suspense no longer.

He went to the stables, saddled Intrepid, and departed at a gallop toward Salters Hall.

=20=

MIMI WAS IN THE ladies' sitting room, gazing out of the window and wondering if it was going to rain, when Waring came in.

"Lord Litton to see you, Miss Mimi."

Mrs. Forbes looked up from her sewing. "I suppose we must receive his lordship in the drawing room," she said, sticking her needle into a singularly ugly garment of dark-brown flannel and beginning to fold it.

"His lordship desires a private word with Miss Mimi, madam."

"With me?" Mimi was aghast. She had never really thought of the viscount as a suitor. Harriet would be brokenhearted if she found out.

"I daresay your father would permit it," said Mrs. Forbes resignedly, "seeing that you have entertained alone every young man for miles this past week. Certainly Lord Litton is the most eligible of them by far, though if he has spoken to the colonel it is more than I have heard. Modern manners!" She unfolded the depressing petticoat again. "Off you go, child."

"But I had rather not, ma'am."

"You must see him, if only to refuse him, my dear. I should never have been permitted to reject so flattering an offer. You are fortunate to have so indulgent a father."

Mimi trailed out, trying desperately to think of something to do or say that would forestall the unwelcome proposal. Her mind was blank.

The viscount was leaning against the mantel, staring into the empty grate. He turned as she entered the room, and came toward her, a remarkably attractive and well set-up figure in an elegant snuff-brown riding coat and cream breeches.

"Miss Lassiter."

Before he could say anything more, she blurted out, "Good day, my lord. Would you like to see my tadpoles? Their legs are fully developed and their tails beginning to shrink."

He looked so disconcerted she wanted to laugh, but ingrained manners came to his rescue. "Thank you, not today, ma'am. Will you not be seated? I . . . I have something most particular to ask of you."

Mimi chose a straight chair near a window and sat stiffly upright, her hands folded in her lap. Botheration! she thought; if she had sat Indian-fashion on the floor he would have found it practically impossible to address her, but she would feel a real ninnyhammer if she moved now.

He stood leaning against the windowsill. Though his features were shadowed, she could make out an expression of embarrassment on his handsome face. He didn't exactly seem eager to make her his bride, she realized with indignation.

"Miss Lassiter, you are in Miss Cooper's confidence, I think?"

A wave of relief washed over her. It *was* Harriet he was interested in. "I am, sir," she agreed cordially, curious as to what was to follow.

With an impatient movement he pulled up a chair beside her. "I know I can trust in your kindness to your friend, and I believe I can also trust in your discretion," he said with unwonted earnestness. He ran his hand through his dark locks, the first time she had ever seen his hair disarranged. "I fear you will think me a coxcomb."

"Possibly." She smiled, and he gave her a rueful grin.

"Deuce take it, this is difficult." Rising abruptly, he took a quick turn about the room, then came back to stand with one hand on the back of his chair, his cheeks flushed. "I want to marry Harriet. Am I foolish to hope that she might one day come to love me?"

"Whyever should she not?" asked Mimi, astonished.

"Oh, I am a frippery fellow, knowing more of fashion than of orphanages, though I do my best to be a good landlord, and son and brother . . ."

"And nephew."

". . . and nephew." He smiled absently. "And if intentions count for anything, I shall be the best husband in the world. She shall lack for nothing that can add to her happiness! Yet I dare hope to be loved for myself, not because I am wealthy and titled."

Mimi looked him straight in the eye and said positively, "Harriet has a soul above such considerations."

The tension visibly seeped out of him. "Yes, of course. I am a coxcomb to have doubted her. Bless you, Miss Lassiter." He took her hand, pressing it lightly as he bowed over it. "Pray excuse me now."

"Good day, sir. I am glad to have been of assistance. Harriet is the dearest girl. You will never regret your choice."

"No, never." He strode to the door, then turned and said in an uncertain voice, "But will she have me?"

There was only one possible answer to that. "Go and ask her," Mimi advised.

Pensive, she watched him go. The London ploy had worked. Yet if Gerald, Viscount Litton, was so unsure of himself, Simon Hurst, without his lordship's manifest advantages, might well lack confidence. Was that why he didn't propose? Or was it pride? Or simply that he wanted nothing more from her than friendship?

Before reflecting on these multitudinous impediments could drive her right into the dismals, Waring appeared at the drawing-room door.

"Mr. Blake requests a private word, miss."

"Oh lord!" Mimi groaned. "Did you inform Mrs. Forbes?"

"Yes, Miss Mimi." The staid butler grinned. "Madam

threw up her hands and demanded to know what the world is coming to. I was unable to give her a satisfactory response, I fear."

"Well, best get it over with. Show him in, Waring, show him in."

Harriet walked down the village street, a laden basket over one arm, Prue's little hand clasped in hers, and Sally skipping alongside. As they passed the green, she remembered the cricket game, her wager with Gerald, the rose-painted fan that was too precious to use. On the other side of the street was Mrs. Mullins's haberdashery, where Mimi had bought the ribbons for the gown she had given Harriet, the one she wore the first time she sang to Gerald.

Lost in memories, she was unaware of the presence of the subject of her thoughts, tying his horse to the vicarage fence, until Prue tugged her hand free and ran to meet him.

Skidding to a halt, she dropped a curtsy. "Hallo, my lord. Did you come to see us? We went shopping and Harriet bought some peppermint bull's-eyes. You can have one if you promise not to tell Mama."

"Lords don't eat sweeties, silly," Sally told her.

"This lord does," said the viscount, his laughing eyes meeting Harriet's over the children's heads.

"So does Papa," Prue assured him earnestly.

"I have come to see your papa." He was not laughing now; indeed, his voice was diffident. "Miss Cooper, do you suppose the vicar could spare me a few minutes?"

"I expect so, sir. Pray come in." Harriet was disappointed. She had hoped he was calling on her, not on parish business.

They escorted him to her father's study, then repaired to the kitchen with the shopping. Leaving it for the cook-maid to put away, Harriet took the paper of bull's-eyes and gave the girls one each.

"Go and fetch your books," she said. "Mama and Judith are out, so you shall read to me while I do some mending in the parlor."

Ten minutes later she was patching a rent in the seat of Jimmy's breeches while Sally, on the sofa beside her, stumbled sticky-tongued through Mr. Charles Lamb's *Adventures of Ulysses*. The enchantress Circe had no sooner turned the hero's crew into swine than Lord Litton came in.

"Off you go, girls," he said cheerfully, "or I shall turn you into frogs. I want a word with your sister."

Harriet scarcely heard their protests as he herded them out. She sat frozen, the torn breeches in her hands, until he gently removed them, sat down beside her, and took her hands in his.

"Marry me, Harriet," he said.

The warmth in his eyes made her blush and lower her gaze, but she had seen anxiety too. "Yes," she breathed, "oh yes."

She could not say more, for he crushed the breath out of her, alternating tender words and tenderer kisses. Putting her arms about his neck, she pressed close to him. He must love her, for no other reason could explain his wanting so ordinary a girl for his wife. But did he understand that she loved him too? She had to be sure he didn't think she would marry him for his title.

Pulling away a little, she took one of his hands and held it to her cheek. "I must tell you, my lord . . ."

"Gerald."

"Gerald," she repeated obediently.

He stroked her other cheek. "Wild roses," he murmured, and bent his head to kiss her again.

"Wait, Gerald. Let me speak. You see, I love you. I tried hard not to, because you are so far above me in station I knew it was hopeless, but I could not help it."

"And it was not hopeless after all." His laugh was joyous. "I fell in love with you at the cricket match, of all places. When you joined in, despite your qualms, to support your friend. No, it was before that, when you asked for a plain, inexpensive fan. Where is it, by the way? I have not seen you use it."

"It is too precious to use. I feared it might be the only thing I had to remember you by."

"You shall have a dozen fans, a hundred, and not a one of them plain or inexpensive."

"I shall still treasure that one."

That statement called for another kiss, which his lordship duly provided.

Emerging at last from his embrace, Harriet said guiltily, "Oh dear, your neckcloth is sadly crushed." She tried to smooth it, but he caught her hands, grinning.

"Do you know when I decided that you would be the perfect wife for me? It was shortly after I fell in love, when you ordered poor Lloyd to guard my coat with his life."

Harriet chuckled, but before she could speak the door was flung open and two grubby boys bounced in.

"Harry . . . Oh, hello, sir . . . Harriet, Sally says you bought some bull's-eyes," cried Jimmy. "Where are they?"

"Hello, sir." Peter bowed and thoughtfully eyed the viscount's arm about his sister's waist, but decided not to mention it for fear of distracting his lordship from serious business. "When will you play cricket with us again?"

The little girls appeared in the doorway. "Sir," begged Sally, "pray tell Prue you won't really turn her into a frog if she comes in."

"You are quite safe, Miss Prudence. I am finished with Harriet . . . for the moment." Gerald arranged a time for a cricket game while Harriet discovered the bull's-eyes under Jimmy's torn breeches.

She admired the way he dealt with the children, but at the moment she would have given anything for a few minutes of peace to consider quietly the amazing fact that he loved and wanted her.

He turned to her and took her hands. "You will want to talk to your parents, I am sure. If I come back in an hour—or two, if you insist—with my curricle, will you go for a drive with me?"

She glanced at the clock on the mantel. "Mama should be back any time now. One hour will be *plenty*."

He kissed her hands, both of them, and then, as if powerless to resist, he folded her in his arms and kissed her full on the mouth right in front of the fascinated children.

"Deuced bad form," he murmured, his eyes laughing, "but I couldn't help it."

"Ahem, Miss Lassiter, I daresay you think me a dry stick of a lawyer, but I assure you I am capable of passion." Mr. Blake folded Mimi in his arms and kissed her full on the mouth.

Mimi kicked him on the shins and pulled away. "Ouch!" She rubbed her sore toes in their thin slippers. "How dare you, sir! I didn't give you permission to maul me."

"Ahem." He straightened his cravat. "Not in so many words, I am prepared to admit, but your behavior has been such as to lead me to believe that my advances would not be unwelcome. Indeed, I have wondered at times whether you are quite suited to become the wife of a professional man such as myself, whose reputation must be beyond doubt in every particular."

"Not at all suited."

"However, my undying devotion has overcome my scruples. Miss Lassiter, be mine!"

As he was advancing on her again with open arms, Mimi was delighted to hear a loud "Ahem!" from another quarter.

"Miss Mimi." Standing in the doorway, Waring announced in his most butlerish voice, "I beg your pardon for interrupting, but there are frogs all over the kitchen, and Cook is throwing forty fits."

Mimi jumped up and sped to his side, where she paused long enough to look back and say, "No, I won't be yours. Good day, sir."

She raced down the passage to the kitchen, slipped through the door, and carefully closed it behind her. Cook stood on the table, her face even redder than usual, directing her troops with a martial air and waving a large carving knife. Jacko, a footman, the bootboy, and the scullery maid, armed with a variety of pots and pans, were skulking about, occasionally pouncing with a triumphant cry of "I got 'im."

Cook spotted Mimi. " 'Tis a good job, miss, as I ben't one o' them French chefs," she said severely, "or I'd have t'legs off 'em quick as milk can curdle."

"I'm sorry, Cook. I meant to take them down to the pond today. I didn't realize they had turned into frogs already. Jacko, look, there's one by your right foot. Don't step on the poor little thing."

One of the tiny creatures leaped to a spot on the red tile floor just in front of her. Stooping swiftly, she picked it up. It sat on her hand, its throat throbbing, looking at her in somewhat confused indignation.

"Well done, miss," the footman congratulated her.

She thought it was rather handsome, with smooth, black-spotted, greenish-brown skin and bright eyes. Most of the tadpole tail protruding between its hind legs had already been absorbed. She should have guessed they were ready to escape from their casserole.

Her captive shifted slightly on her palm and she clapped her other hand over it. "Where shall I put it?" she asked.

"Got a bucket wi' a cover in the scullery, Miss Mimi," said Jacko. "I a'ready catched all of 'em in there. Just be careful when you takes that cover off to put 'im in."

Watching every step, she went out to the scullery. On the draining board, beside the empty casserole, was a bucket with a loose-fitting metal lid. She raised the lid an inch and stuffed her frog through the gap. A muffled croaking arose.

Soon all the fugitives were rounded up and transferred to the bucket. "I'd better take them to the pond right away," Mimi said to Jacko. "They are horridly crowded in there. I'll just go and change my shoes."

"I'll take 'em for you, miss."

"Thank you, but I shall enjoy the walk, and the bucket is not too heavy." She had had enough excitement for one day. A stroll through the gardens would be soothing.

The heavy clouds were breaking up, the summer sun shining warmly through the blue gaps between. It seemed silly to wear hat and gloves for the sake of convention when she was doing something as unconventional as carrying a bucket full of frogs. With Rohan dashing about her heels, she paused to admire the flowers, exchanging a few words with a gardener who was weeding the rose beds.

As she approached the ha-ha, her footsteps slowed. Somehow, releasing the frogs would be the end of a chapter. Her acquaintance with Simon had begun with the tadpoles. He had helped her care for them and taken an interest in their development; she wished he was going to be with her when she let them go.

She wished the proposed London Season had worked on him as powerfully as it appeared to have worked on Gerald. Wistfully, she wondered whether Harriet was even now clasped in the viscount's arms. Starting down the ha-ha steps, she was lost in a dream in which Simon held her close—and for once neither of them was soaking wet.

Rohan barked. Startled, Mimi stumbled. In saving herself she dropped the bucket. It hit the stone steps with a clang and tipped over, the lid falling off. From it poured a stream of frogs, hopping, leaping, croaking in joy as they caught the heavenly smell of pond. In an instant they reached the bottom of the steps and bounded across the grass toward the water—right under Intrepid's nose.

With a snort of alarm the gelding reared. Mimi had no sooner realized that Simon was there than he was thrown. His hat flew off, his head met the ha-ha wall with a thud, and he lay still.

Simon rose through layers of hazy consciousness. His head hurt, but otherwise he was quite comfortable, lying on something warm and soft. He opened his eyes.

Gazing up into worried black eyes, he made no effort to remove his person from Mimi's lap.

"Simon! At last! Are you all right?"

"Never felt better," he said dreamily. "Will you marry me, Princess?"

For answer she bent her head and kissed him. Her lips on his were even warmer and softer than her lap.

"I wish I'd kept my promise sooner," she said.

"No matter now." He reached up and ran his fingers down the curve of her smooth brown cheek. "You have broken the spell at last."

She giggled. "You mean you have turned into a prince? You don't look any different."

"Not quite a prince. Merely an earl, but I'm going to be a marquis."

"You are quizzing me."

"Not at all. I'm Gerald's cousin, Earl of Derwent and heir to the Marquis of Stokesbury. Do you mind, love?"

"Mind? Good heavens no. Does that mean you are rich?"

"Moderately. I shall be very rich one day."

"So you don't care about my dowry."

"It's you I want, Princess. I wouldn't give a sailor's curse for your fortune."

"I'm glad." She kissed him again, in a thoughtful way. "Then you won't mind if I give it back to Papa to found another orphanage?"

He began to laugh, which hurt his head so that he groaned. That required several more kisses to cure, and they were thus pleasantly engaged when a loud "Halloo" interrupted them.

Rohan barked a warning as Gerald rode up, leading Intrepid with Henry clinging to the saddle. The little valet slipped thankfully to the ground.

"My lord, thank heaven you are safe! I was hanging out your shirts to dry when your horse galloped past me alone."

"Nothing would calm the man but that I bring him with me to find you," drawled Gerald. "Deuced bad form, you know, old fellow, lying in a lady's lap in public."

"It wasn't public a moment ago," Mimi pointed out.

"She's not a lady, she's a princess, and I'm going to marry her. You should try it some time, coz."

"I shall. I am going to marry Harriet Cooper."

Mimi clapped her hands. "That's splendid!"

"Another of your plots?" Simon asked suspiciously.

"Of course. All my projects always turn out for the best."

Gerald laughed. "I'm in no position to quarrel with that, ma'am. Am I to take it, coz, that you have informed your betrothed of your true rank?"

"Say rather that she has restored me to it." A look of understanding passed between the two cousins. Lady Elizabeth's cruel enchantment was finished and to be forgotten. Simon would never again doubt his own worth.

"My lord, my lord!" Henry sank to his knees beside them in his excitement. "I may serve you again? I may send for your trunks?"

"Good gad, no! I mean, yes you may serve me, but I'll be damned if I'm going to let you torture me with fashion again."

"A few alterations," the valet murmured hopefully.

"I trust you do not mean to continue to offend my eyes with the appalling garments you have been wearing these past weeks?" Gerald demanded.

"They're not appalling!" Mimi flared up in defense of her beloved. "Simon shall wear what he wants and be comfortable."

"Thank you, my love. Now do go away, you two." Simon made a shooing gesture. "My princess and I have some unfinished business to complete. Where were we?"

"You were about to say that Papa can have my fortune for an orphanage," Mimi reminded him as Gerald and Henry departed.

"Was I?"

"Yes." Her kiss was most persuasive.

"All right, I'll make a bargain. I shall forgo your dowry if you promise that when we are married you will perform your scandalous Indian dance for me."

Her eyes lit with a familiar spark of mischief. "Oh yes," she said, "I promise. Let's get married soon!"

If you would like to receive details on other Walker Regency romances, please write to:

The Regency Editor
Walker and Company
720 Fifth Avenue
New York, NY 10019